Dustin's Endless Love

Seven Giants Series: Book Three

MzSassytheAuthor

Dustin's Endless Love

Copyright © 2020 by MzSassytheAuthor.

This book is a work of fiction. Names, characters, businesses, organiza- tions, places, events, and incidents either are the product of the author's imagination or are used fictitiously. Any resemblance to actual persons, living or dead, events, or locales is entirely coincidental.

Contact the Author:
mzsassytheauthor@gmail.com

Instagram: mzsassytheauthor

Facebook.com/mzsassytheauthor

Twitter: mzsassytheauth1

Book and Cover design by:
Amethyst Phoenix Press

First Edition: December 2020
ISBN: 9781736972274

Chapter One

Nadia Bolton shot upright in her bed, placing her hand on her chest in an attempt to calm her erratic heartbeat. She looked over at her fiancé peacefully sleeping and slightly snoring, completely oblivious to the jolt of the bed as she extracted herself from the dream she was having. Slowly pulling the sheet from over her legs, she quietly left the bed, tiptoed over to the connecting bathroom, and closed the door softly. She leaned against the door, resting her head back against it and closed her eyes. Three days. That's how long she'd been having the same dream. She was sitting but didn't know where. She heard noises but couldn't make out what they were. It sounded like heavy breathing or a puffing of breath. Her eyes had been closed, and she felt strong warm arms surrounding her. She leaned in, loving the comfort they brought. Resting her head back on strong shoulders, she exhaled, knowing she felt the safest she'd ever been. Feeling a chin rub against the side of her face, making her smile, and turning in to receive the kiss she knew awaited her. Slowly opening her eyes, she yearned to connect with the brown eyes of her fiancé, but when she opened them, she connected with gray ones. The shock of that alone woke her up.

Now, here she was again after scaring herself awake and fleeing to the bathroom, trying to calm her nerves. Moving away from the bathroom door, she walked over to the sink. Staring at herself in the mirror with guilt looking back at her. The first two nights, she'd immediately awaken, fearing what would happen if she stayed asleep. However, last night, she'd taken the bait and allowed the kiss to happen. Instantly, the kiss vibrated through every cell in her body as if it knew it would only come to life with this man. How could it feel so real, so perfect? It was only a dream. And how could she dream of enjoying another man's arms, accepting another man's kiss, with her fiancé sleeping right beside her.

She soon would become Mrs. Kyle Franklin. The envy of everyone in the Black Coalition Group of Houston and the future wife of a senator. She'd met Kyle three years ago at the children's hospital that she volunteered at. Many suffered from memory loss as she had, and she wanted to comfort them and reassure them that life could still be good after a tragedy like that. She knew it was more so for herself than for the kids. Kyle was visiting at a routine stop for his campaign. He invited her to lunch, seemed completely unbothered by her lack of memory, and the rest was history. Twelve years ago, she'd woken up in a hospital room in a small medical center outside Houston. She remembered a nurse asking her several times what her name was, and she couldn't remember. It was the scariest thing in the world. She didn't know her name, her age, or her birthdate. Her body ached all over, and the smell of what seemed like burnt flesh trickled into her nostrils. She was lucky to be alive. She'd flatlined twice according to what the doctors told her. Turning on the water to wash away some of the flush in her cheeks, she was puzzled, trying to understand what was happening to her.

"**You only** have 20 minutes before the ceremony starts. I don't think you can make it." Donnell said as Dustin settled in his helicopter.

"Do you know where she is right now?"

"The limo just left the boutique."

"Is there any way you can stall?" Donnell knew exactly what Dustin was referring to.

"I'm not breaking into the Houston Traffic Authority, Dustin."

"I just need a little bit of time, Donnie."

"I'll see what I can do." Dustin said his thanks to Donnell and lifted off in his helicopter. He knew he was making a daring move and that his interruption would probably be unwelcomed. But it wasn't every day you found out your dead wife was very much alive and about to marry someone else. He couldn't believe his eyes when he'd seen her three weeks ago, at his friend Dominic Blake's baby shower. He thought it was strange that the baby shower was held after the baby was born. According to Dominic, the media had gotten wind of the gender reveal and caused Ashiree to forego any additional events until after the baby was born. Dustin could understand that. He wasn't big on being in the spotlight, either. Ashiree introduced Nadia Bolton to him. Once he could get his mind over the shock of seeing her, he told Dominic and their friend Donnell, the woman he'd just seen, was not Nadia Bolton but his supposedly dead wife, Tricia Hanson.

Almost an hour later, Dustin landed his helicopter on the X marked on the top of the closest downtown building to the church. A few men assisted him through the building down to the street. He checked his watch, and he was pretty certain the ceremony was starting. He could run the ten blocks to the church, but he hadn't considered that when he decided to wear his boots. He noticed a horse and buggy across the street and smiled. A horse he could do. Negotiating with the driver to let him borrow the horse, he galloped down the downtown streets of Houston, ignoring the stares, car horns, and walking pedestrians. He had to get to the church, and he had a feeling he was already out of time. His mind took him back to when he'd first seen her...

Dustin age twelve:

The car door slammed, and Dustin watched the dust from the wheels spurt up as the car took off.

"Don't be in our way, you little runt."

"Yeah, and don't tell anyone you know us, either." Dustin picked up his duffle bag as he watched his brothers

Jacob and Matthew walk over to greet their friends. Jacob was the oldest, four years his senior, and Matthew was a year behind. Dustin slumped his shoulders and walked through the grassy pathway to his cabin. The campsite had one main walkway separating the girl cabins from the boys and at the very end was a stable and the lake. There were plenty of chaperones giving instructions, welcoming everyone to a wonderful summer and encouraging them all to make new friends. Dustin couldn't even be friends with his own brothers. How was he supposed to do it with strangers? Each cabin was selected by age group, so Jacob and Matthew would be two cabins away from him. Entering his cabin, he found the last bunk in the back and placed his bag on the floor next to it. It smelled like sweaty old socks and spoiled underwear. He was pretty sure the Texas heat wouldn't make it any better. Two whole months of this smell. He breathed out a sigh and laid back on the mattress of the bottom bunk. Resting his head on his hands, he looked at the bottom of the upper bunk. In the wood was carved the words "Tricia Hanson was here." He arched a brow. Tricia sounded like a girl's name. What was the engraving doing on a bunk in the boys' cabin?

"You're one brave soul?" He looked over to see another boy claiming the bottom bunk next to his. Dustin sat up.

"What do you mean?"

"No one has slept in that bunk in the last three summers." The boy said, taking out his sheets to cover the bed before sitting on it.

"Why not?"

"Do you see that stitch right there?" He said, pointing to the beam with the engraving.

"Yes, so what?" Dustin said, shrugging his shoulders.

"Well, the legend is that it's cursed."

"Spreading stupid rumors around again, Patrick." Another cabin member said, taking the bunk across from them.

"Hey, I'm just trying to help him out." The other boy shook his head while dropping his bag on the floor. He walked over and extended his hand to Dustin.

"Hey. I'm Oscar, and this idiot is Patrick. " He said while throwing his head toward who Dustin now knew was Patrick.

"I'm Dustin," He said, accepting Oscar's hand.

"First year?" Oscar asked.

"Yeah." He said nervously. So many things were changing in his life, and it was hard to keep up with.

"Well, don't let this fool scare you. Your bed isn't cursed, but he's not completely wrong to warn you. That girl..." he said, pointing to the name on the beam. "...you do want to stay away from." With that warning, Oscar went back over to his side and began to make his bed up. Seeing both boys placing their sheets on the bed, Dustin decided to do the same. Once his bed was made, and a few of his clothes were put on the tiny dresser next to the bed, a commotion was heard outside the cabin, and then a boy came in yelling.

"FIGHT!!!" The other boys rushed out of the cabin, and Dustin followed. It was the first day of camp, and already there was a fight. Leaving the cabin, he followed the other boys, practically running to the scene where a small crowd gathered. Ooh and ahh sounds resonated throughout the crowd as they watched the fight before them. Dustin shoved his way to get to the edge of the action and stood next to Oscar and Patrick.

"There is no way Ethan's going to win this year."

"I don't know. He grew an inch since last summer." Dustin heard a few boys say while watching the two fighters. One was wearing a baseball cap and was clearly smaller than the other guy named Ethan. Ethan ducked past a punch and grabbed the other fighter from behind. With a short holler, the fighter quickly planted their feet, hunched over, and sent Ethan flying over them, landing flat on his back.

"Yield!" they yelled, placing their foot on Ethan's chest. Dustin watched as Ethan surrendered his hands in defeat. Cheers, as well as mumbles and grumbles, were heard in the crowd.

"Man, I thought Ethan had her this year." He heard a boy say while walking away. Did he just say her? Dustin looked back at the fighters as the winner helped Ethan off the ground.

"That's a girl?" Dustin stated out loud to no one in particular.

"That's not just a girl, that's *the* girl." Patrick answered him. Dustin looked back over as the fighters appeared to talk like best friends.

"You have to be kidding me."

"Nope." Oscar said, clapping his arm on Dustin's shoulder.

"That's Tricia Hanson."

Chapter Two

Nadia stood with the other ladies in the room while several of the bridal party assisted her in getting dressed, as the time had come for the wedding to begin. Mrs. Franklin was giving instructions to the wedding planner, as she always had. Nadia had not been involved in planning her own wedding. The entire ordeal made her feel out of place. Colors, place settings, or even a seating chart. She didn't have the answers for any of it. She wondered if every bride felt this uncertain on their wedding day. As the ladies started to line up in front of her, Fiona Childs came to stand beside her.

"How are you holding up? Are you excited?" Nadia smiled, unsure of how she felt. She honestly didn't know how to answer Fiona's question.

"I'm a little nervous." She said, downplaying the true fear rising in her. She was getting married with no family or close friends. The only associations she had were the people at her job and those associated with Kyle in some form or another, like Fiona. When she and Kyle began dating, Fiona and another woman named Margery Pitts began inviting her into their fold. Fiona was around her height of 5'5' and body shape. Full of curves and ample in the breast department, while Margery was tall, slender and could put most runway models to shame. Fiona was kind, strait-laced and married to Kyle's cousin, a dentist, and they had a little girl. Margery was single, slightly shallow, and frequently made Nadia feel uncomfortable around her. The association with them was at the request of Kyle's mother. Kyle was on the path to becoming a Senator, needing the right connections, image, and wife. Nadia wasn't sure how she fit into the right wife category, especially not knowing anything about her life beyond the last twelve years.

"Don't worry. All brides are nervous on their wedding day. Just think about the very handsome man waiting for you at the end of the aisle." Fiona smiled, giving Nadia a light pat on her hands that were folded in front of her. Nadia closed her eyes as she took a deep breath, attempting to conjure up Kyle's face waiting for her in the church sanctuary. Imagining him standing there, black shoes, black pants, white shirt underneath his black jacket, she could almost picture his brown eyes coming to view, but the eyes she imagined weren't brown. They were gray. His face, neck and hands weren't brown; they were white. The image she saw in her mind wasn't of Kyle at all. It was him. The rugged cowboy she'd met before leaving Ashiree Blake's baby shower.

The music in the church began, and she opened her eyes, noticing the wedding party was now entering the sanctuary in the proper order and timing as directed by the wedding planner. Inhaling and exhaling slowly, she closed her eyes, and there he was again. She didn't understand why the image of this man plagued her mind. For almost three weeks, he invaded her thoughts. Especially at night, when controlling her mind was impossible. He wasn't even nice to her. She was about to leave the baby shower when Ashiree introduced them. He didn't even have the courtesy to shake her hand. He just stood there, staring at her. Determined not to let the situation embarrass her, she plastered on a smile, said her goodbyes and quickly left. She didn't understand why her brain chose to focus on him constantly. Sensing the movement of the flower girls in front of her, she opened her eyes again and stepped forward. Kyle's uncle slowly slid his arm through hers, startling her just a little.

"Are you alright, my dear?" He asked in his husky southern drawl. She shook her head no. He chuckled slightly beside her and patted her arm. He was kind enough to volunteer to walk her down the aisle.

"It's perfectly natural to be nervous. Most people are on their wedding day." He said, trying to reassure her. She smiled the best she could, took a deep breath and then exhaled as the wedding march song began.

Dustin brought the horse to a stop in front of the church and hopped off. He patted the horse, thanking him, and began running up the stairs to the cathedral church. Hearing the Bridal Chorus playing, he knew he had to hurry. Once he entered the church, he was stopped by two men in black suits.

"Bride or Groom?"

"Bride." Dustin answered, annoyed that he was being delayed even more. He watched the men share a look as they looked over his shoulder, noticing he'd arrived on horseback.

"Do you have your invitation, sir?"

"No." The man with a tablet in his hand asked for his name." He knew he wasn't on the registry. So, there was no surprise that his name wasn't on the list.

"I'm sorry, sir, we can't let you in."

"I have to get in. It's very important."

"I'm sorry, sir, but without an invitation...."

"Dustin?" He almost breathed a sigh of relief as he saw Ashiree walking over to the entryway of the church, carrying a baby in her arms.

"Ashiree. I don't have my invitation." He said in a tone that he hoped conveyed to her he needed help. He'd had spent little time with his friend's wife well enough to know if she would catch on. She walked over and addressed the men.

"He's my plus one. You'll find my name on your list. Ashiree Blake." At the mention of the Blake name, both men seemed tense while searching the guest list and then nodded their approval to allow Dustin entrance.

"You are a lifesaver." He whispered as they walked away from the men.

"Or you're just lucky Arion began to fuss." That prompted Dustin to look down at the bundle she was carrying. The newest edition to the Blake family was staring right back at him with a pacifier in his mouth.

"Where is Dominic?"

"He's in Boston, helping with some issues at Jacen's new club." Dustin nodded as they walked further into the church. He was aware of Dominic's family having connections to a Boston family that went by the last name Turner. He had met none of them, but he knew they were a part of helping Dominic find Ashiree when she'd been kidnapped last year. If he recalled, Ashiree was best friends with Jacen's wife.

"I'm surprised you're not with him."

"I didn't want to miss Nadia's wedding." She paused, eyeing him suspiciously, before continuing. "Which it appears I will be, anyway." She said teasingly. Dustin looked at her, confusingly until recognition dawned on him.

"You talk to Donnie?"

"He texted shortly after I arrived." Dustin nodded. "You're cutting it a bit close, aren't you?" She asked.

"You mean you're not going to try to stop me?" She shook her head.

"Which door is the sanctuary?" She pointed to the one on the left. He took a deep breath and began walking toward the double doors, just as another memory invaded his mind.

Dustin at fifteen:

Dustin dusted off the muck on his jeans as he exited the stable. This was his first summer at camp without his brothers. They ignored him when they were here anyway, but this summer would be different. He was actually different. Gone was the scrawny twelve-year-old who had arrived three years ago and some of the last summer. Now he was almost full grown. Standing tall at six feet and potentially more to grow. His body definitely changed. Scrawny arms? You wouldn't find those. Skinny legs? No, you wouldn't find those either. Last year, he joined the wrestling team and built up perfectly placed muscles on his body. He wasn't shallow or bragging, but he'd worked hard to look and feel as strong as he was. With two older brothers that seemed to use him as a punching bag anytime, their father wasn't looking. Becoming stronger was a means to survive.

Looking up at the sky, he couldn't spot a single cloud. It was going to be a very hot day. Resting on the side of the stable door with one leg crossed and his arms folded, he thought about his mom. He hadn't seen her in four years and missed her. The calls to her grew further and less frequent. She was convinced he wasn't safe in Cancun anymore and sent him to live with his father. He could count on one hand how many times he'd seen his father until he came to live with him. He was the secret child or, better yet, the illegitimate child of Preston David Shaw. At least that's what he heard others say regarding him when they assumed he couldn't hear them, or more so when they assumed his father couldn't hear them. Matthew and Jacob practically ignored him unless they were fighting. Lately, girls had been their focus. Dustin was more reserved around the opposite sex. Girls were weird to him. Matthew and Jacob dated girls so concerned about makeup and clothes and went completely crazy when they broke up with them. Matthew's last girlfriend superglued the keyholes in his car over winter break. Crazy. Who even thinks of that? Dustin didn't get girls and pretty much kept his distance if he could. But horses, now that was a different thing. Even now, standing in the doorway of the stable, he could hear the slight neighing of the horses as if they were complaining about the heat also.

Last summer, they had been his fascination when neither Oscar nor Patrick returned to camp. Since Jacob did not come due to him graduating and heading off to college, Matthew took every opportunity to taunt him. He'd come to the stable barn to blow off some steam and embarrassment and almost collided with the Horse Wrangler Brett. Seeming to understand Dustin's plight to get away, he allowed him in the stable to seek some solace. In return, Dustin had to work. He didn't mind mucking out the stalls because, in return, he was able to feed the horses, brush them and bond with them. His favorites were twins. It was rare that two horses would survive such an occurrence. Hansel and Gretel. He thought the names fit them. A commotion at the lake brought Dustin out of his thoughts as he narrowed his eyes. A girl was being tossed up and dunked in the lake. Others were laughing and then someone was running from the lake. He heard shouting as the boy ran toward Dustin, holding something in his hand.

"Stop him." He heard someone shout. Dustin moved off the stable door to stop the boy, but he was looking behind him and ran smack into Dustin. Dustin caught his footing, but the boy slipped and fell flat on his face, dropping the item in his hand. Dustin picked it up, not surprised it was a girl's bikini top. The boy on the ground muttered a curse word and turned over. Dustin recognized him. Holding the bikini top by his finger, he looked down at him.

"I'm not sure this is your style or your color, Jack." Dustin said. Jack reached for his leg, which was scraped and bleeding.

"When did you become a brick wall, Dusty?"

"Well, if it isn't Dusty Roads." Dustin turned, instantly recognized Chad's voice. Chad was the culprit with Matthew last summer, trying to make his life a living hell.

"Chad." Dustin addressed him dryly. He folded his arms, not at all concerned with the bikini top hanging from his finger.

"Why don't you just give that to me?" He said, pointing to the bikini top.

"Doesn't seem like your style or color, either."

"It doesn't matter, and it doesn't belong to you."

"I'm sure it doesn't belong to you either." Dustin responded. By this time, most of the kids from the lake were watching the stare down between him and Chad. Jack was still moaning on the ground about his knee, but no one was paying attention.

"Oh! You think you are big and bad now, since your brother isn't here to keep you in check." Dustin strengthened his stance. Not bothering to respond. He'd grown a full six inches in the last year, and his confidence level was much higher. He stood an inch taller than Chad now, but Chad had him in body mass. Not that it mattered. He took down guys bigger than Chad in the wrestling rink with ease. Chad reached for the bikini top, and Dustin swiftly moved his arms apart to keep it out of his reach. There were a few chuckles in the crowd. Chad looked back at the other kids with a smirk, but Dustin anticipated his next move. The moment Chad chose to strike, Dustin moved quickly, dodging Chad's punch. Chad caught his footing as he hadn't suspected not connecting his fist to Dustin's face. Red hot anger lined in his jaw. He took two more swings at Dustin. Both times he missed. The last jab,

Dustin caught in his own hand, shocking the crowd and Chad as well. Seeing his hand caught in Dustin's, a flash of panic appeared on Chad's face, right before Dustin's other hand fisted and connected with his jaw, sending Chad down flat on his back. Chad grumbled, complaining about his nose. Dustin ignored him and bent down to pick up the bikini top he'd dropped during the fight. He only had to wonder for a second whose top it was.

"I think that belongs to me." Dustin heard. He looked up, bikini top now in his hand, into the big brown eyes of Tricia Hanson. She was standing with a towel wrapped around her, her hand out, anger clearly seeping through her pores. He dusted the few specks of dirt off the top and handed it to her. She snatched it and walked past him to Chad, who was getting up off the ground still holding his nose.

"You thought your little joke was funny." She said to Chad, who was laughing with a bleeding nose.

"Hey, you grew a nice rack. Can't blame a guy for wanting to see." Chad's comment caused laughter by a few in the crowd. Dustin was ready to hit him again. He never got the chance to move before Tricia kicked Chad in the balls. Causing him to holler and every guy around to instantly flinch. If girls really knew how painful that was, they would stop doing it.

"Laugh at that." She scuffed as Chad was now back on the ground, holding his junk. Counselors and Chaperones were now hurrying over, noticing the crowd and the wailing of both Chad and Jack.

"Tricia, we have to go?" He heard a girl say, trying to grab Tricia's arm. "You can't afford to get in trouble again."

"They're going to know something as soon as they see me in this towel."

"You can hide in the stable." Dustin suggested before he knew what he was saying. Kids were not normally allowed in the stable, but Brett had made an exception for him. Both girls nodded and ran into the stables to hide. Dustin casually closed one door and waited inside for the commotion to die down.

"You can put your top back on over there." He said, pointing to an empty stall close to where they were standing. Tricia walked into the stall, turning her nose up, most likely to the smell. Dustin was used to it by now, but at first, it reeked. Tricia stared back at him, and he wondered for a second if she was so concerned with the condition of the stable that she wouldn't put her top back on. He saw her place her hands on her hips.

"Could you at least turn around?"

"Oh, sorry." He felt embarrassed. Of course, that was her reason for stalling. Turning his back to give her what privacy he could. He was now facing Tricia's friend.

"I'm Tanya." She said with a flirty grin, extending her hand.

"Dustin." He said, taking it, noticing she wasn't quick to let his hand go.

"It's nice to meet you, Dustin. Is this your first year at camp?"

"No, Tanya, he's Matthew and Jacob's little brother." Tricia said, joining them. He hadn't heard her approach, but her appearance allowed him to get his hand back. Tanya was cute, proudly displaying her soft pink bikini.

"We should get out of here." Tricia said, annoyance laced in her voice. He didn't know if it was the lake incident or the obvious flirting with him by Tanya.

"Maybe we'll see you around, Dustin." Tanya said, as Tricia practically booted her out of the stable.

"Maybe." She winked at him, and he once again rested against the door panel as they walked away. He'd focused his eyes on Tanya to keep from looking at what he truly wanted to. He now knew exactly why Chad and Jack pulled their little prank. Tricia was stacked in the breast department. Tanya was slender from top to bottom, perky breast, small waist, slim hips, but Tricia, the complete opposite. Her breasts were also perky but three times the size of Tanya, and so were her hips. She had what his dad would call a coca-cola bottle figure. He honestly hadn't fully understood what that meant until this very moment. He smiled to himself, thinking Tricia was hot.

Chapter Three

Nadia calmed her nerves as she finally made it down the aisle to stand next to Kyle. The minute she began walking to the wedding chorus, she noticed Ashiree in the back on her left, rocking a very aggravated baby, Arion. Ashiree smiled and mouthed *'You look beautiful'*, causing Nadia to say a silent thank you and turn to focus on Kyle. However, her mind was playing tricks on her again. As she continued down the aisle toward Kyle, it wasn't his face she saw. Gray eyes seemed to stare back at her, and she had to blink a few times just to focus. Kyle's uncle kissed her cheek, telling her congratulations. She watched as he took a seat in the front row, and Kyle reached for her hands as the minister began the ceremony. She did her very best to continue looking at Kyle, smiling and convincing herself this was what she wanted. Why wouldn't it be? Every woman wanted to get married, have a family, and live the fairytale life they dreamed of. The problem was she didn't know if this was her fairytale coming to life. She didn't even know if she dreamed of fairytales as a little girl. Could she get married and continue with her life when more than half of it was a total blank? She felt Kyle shake her hands to show her to pay attention. Blinking, she hadn't realized the minister spoke to her.

"I'm sorry. Can you say that again?" She felt Kyle's grip on her hands tighten and heard murmuring amongst those in attendance. Even the minister's brow hunched for a second, but he took a breath and repeated the words to her.

"Do you, Nadia Bolton, take this man, to be your lawfully wedded husband, to have and to hold, for better or for worse, for richer or for poorer, in sickness and in health, to love, honor and cherish, till death do you part." Nadia took a deep breath and looked up to see a very encouraging smile from Kyle.

"I...I..."

"I object." A deep and baritone voice vibrated throughout the church. Nadia turned with Kyle, still holding her hands as her eyes connected with the gray eyes she tried to forget.

"Excuse me." Kyle practically shouted.

"I said I object." The tall man was now approaching the altar where they were standing. Dressed in a navy blue t-shirt, dark jeans and cowboy boots. His stride was confident as he stepped closer to the altar. Nadia focused for the first time on his face. His smooth cream-colored skin, dark hair cropped at the base of his neck, slightly thin lips, and a five o'clock shadow covered his chin.

"What is the meaning of this?" Kyle's mother demanded. Kyle's mother and uncle both stood as well as a few others in the sanctuary.

"Who are you? What gives you the right to interrupt and object at my wedding?" Kyle's voice sounded threatening. Nadia couldn't move as the man stood before her, never taking his eyes off of her.

"This woman isn't free to get married." He said, still looking directly into her eyes. They were so intense, and Nadia did all she could to focus on breathing. What did his words mean?

"What do you mean she's not free? Nadia, do you know him?" Taking her eyes off the man standing in front of them, she shook her head in response to Kyle, unable to find her voice.

"This is ridiculous." Someone in the crowd said, but Nadia averted her eyes to her hands still holding Kyle's. She didn't understand what was going on.

"Young man, I will need you to provide a valid claim as to your objection to these nuptials." The minister said.

"This woman isn't Nadia Bolton." He spoke with such confidence.

"And how do you know that?" Kyle said, finally releasing her hands. Anger and embarrassment were etching his words. She looked over at the man who still hadn't taken his eyes off of her as he reached into his jacket and pulled open a document, handing it to the minister.

"Because her name is Tricia Hanson-Shaw. She's my wife." Nadia's eyes widened at his words. Kyle's mother began to ascend the altar to look at whatever this man...or her husband had given the minister. Panic and anxiety began to rise in her. She tried to slow her breathing, tried to catch her breath as tiny dots formed in her head. Someone called her name, but she saw nothing but gray eyes until everything else went black.

Dustin leaned against the wall as a nurse attempted to wake Nadia. After catching her from falling, which her fiancé wasn't too happy about, he was led to a room in the back of the church. It seemed to be used for storage. There were spare chairs and church pews stacked up. He ended up laying Nadia on one. The groom's family talked in low voices and sent death stares his way. None of it bothered him. His focus was on Nadia. He asked his friend Donnell, a tech genius, to do some digging into Tricia's death when he'd seen her at the baby shower. He thought he had been looking at a ghost, thought his eyes were playing tricks on him. He'd been so caught off guard that he'd practically ignored the introduction Ashiree had made when Nadia was standing right in front of him. Donnell called him this morning, claiming he found discrepancies in the description of Tricia based on the morgue reports from the hospital that did the autopsy. Twelve years ago, a fifty-car pile-up accident was caused by an oil tanker spinning out of control, spilling oil all over the highway and catching fire. Dustin remembered it well, making national news, but he dismissed watching the story. There had been no reason to think Tricia had been on the highway. Her parents told him she had been pronounced dead at the scene amongst several other victims. Donnell discovered a young woman fitting Tricia's description was sent to a nearby medical center a few miles away. Why she wasn't sent to the hospital with the other survivors was still unknown. But she'd stayed there three weeks and suffered from complete memory loss. Donnell followed the trail of her life, leading her right into working at Gateway Pharmaceuticals, the same place Dominic's wife Ashiree worked. He could come up with several streams of good luck or fate working to bring her back into his life, but it was no doubt to Dustin who she was. The door to the room practically burst open as Ashiree came walking in. She instantly walked over to Dustin with a small baby carrier draped over her shoulder.

"Oh my goodness, Dustin, is she alright?"

"They're trying to wake her up now." He said, never taking his eyes off Nadia.

"I'm glad you were there to catch her." Ashiree added.

"He wouldn't have needed to if he hadn't shocked her." Kyle said, his voice lacing with anger. Dustin could understand his anger, but he simply shrugged his shoulders.

"You know we will check the documents you provided to ensure they are accurate." Dustin assumed the woman who spoke was Kyle's mother.

"I certainly hope you do."

"Where the hell have you been the last twelve years if this is your wife?" Kyle barked.

"Kyle, please don't swear in the house of the Lord."

"Give it a rest, mother. You barely go to church." Kyle's mother looked slightly taken back by his words.

"I think we should just focus on Nadia right now."

"And who exactly are you?" Kyle asked, beginning to march over to where Ashiree and Dustin stood. He didn't make it three steps before he was grabbed by the arm and thrust onto the wall next to them.

"What the hell?" Kyle shouted, with his face pressed against the wall.

"Sean!" Ashiree said, almost embarrassed. She hadn't even seen him enter the room.

"If I were you, I would take your hands off that boy right now." Said the older gentlemen standing next to Kyle's mother. Either Sean didn't hear him, or he chose to ignore him.

"Let me go right now." Kyle demanded.

"Sean, please let him go. I don't think he was trying to hurt me." Sean's muscles relaxed as he moved Kyle off the wall, releasing him, then stood in front of Ashiree. Kyle looked as if he wanted to charge at Sean, but he thought better of it, taking in his size and physique.

"Who are you?" Kyle demanded. Sean stood with his arms folded in a military stance. Ashiree took a slight step to his side, but not in front of him.

"Sorry, this is my bodyguard. You were too close to me." Ashiree tried to explain.

"Why do you need a bodyguard?" Kyle's mother asked, now coming to stand next to Kyle.

"My husband's very protective." Ashiree stated.

"And who exactly is your husband?"

"What is this? An interrogation?" Dustin interrupted. The three of them now had a stare down with Kyle's family.

"He attacked me." Kyle accused, pointing at Sean, whose posture still had not shifted.

"You were stalking over toward a woman with a baby. Nobody knew what your intentions were."

"I would never hurt a woman and her child." Kyle said, disgusted with the insinuation.

"Well, he's paid to protect her, no matter what your motives were." Dustin said. Before Kyle could speak, they all turned to the sound of someone's voice.

"Kyle." Nadia said weakly. Dustin's muscles tensed in hearing her wake up and call for Kyle. He knew she didn't know him, but it still bothered him. Watching Kyle kneel down next to her, taking her hand and seeing about her well-being, brought jealousy in him he hadn't expected. He'd spent twelve long years thinking she was dead, and now more than anything, he wanted to touch her, hold her, have her look at him in the way she was now looking at Kyle. She began to sit up, recognition mirrored her face when she saw him, but beyond that, he could tell she had no clue who he was.

"I'm so happy you're awake. Are you alright?" Ashiree said, slowly walking over to Nadia. Sean's movements matched hers, and Kyle stood and took a slight step back. Dustin tried not to let the smirk he held inside display on his face. Kyle was probably a good guy, but Dustin couldn't help but not like him.

"I think I'm alright." He saw her lean slightly over to connect eyes with him.

"You." She said in a confused tone.

"Me." Dustin answered.

"You crashed my wedding." She said in an accusing tone, but not angrily.

"I did." He said flatly.

"You said we were married."

"We are."

"You were rude to me." She stated. Dustin did his best not to smile. He had been rude to her, or at least he understood why she perceived their first meeting that way.

"I thought you said you didn't know him." Kyle interjected. He watched Nadia wince at Kyle's accusing tone. Ashiree spoke before he could.

"They met at my baby shower or reunited, I guess is a better way of saying it."

"You're Dominick Blake's wife?" Kyle asked, astonishment in his voice. Dustin saw Ashiree roll her eyes and nod. He did his best not to laugh. There was no secret who Dominic Blake was, especially in Houston. Nadia began to rise from the pew, and Kyle could get over his shock long enough to assist her in standing. Dustin stood next to Ashiree, causing Nadia to look up at him.

"I apologize." He said, extending his hand to her. Remembering she had done the same to him when Ashiree introduced them at the baby shower, but he had been in a complete state of shock seeing her and had not taken her hand. She took it slowly, and he lightly shook it.

"Hopefully, you can forgive me. It's not every day you see your wife that you thought was dead, standing in front of you." She nodded and pulled her hand slowly away from his.

"I can see how that can be a bit of a shock." She responded shyly. Dustin could see she was nervous and uncomfortable. The tension in the room was like a cold brisk of wind. Baby Arion began to fuss, and Dustin's mind traveled yet again to another memory of them.

Dustin at fifteen:

Dustin slowly brushed Gretel in the stable. After the fiasco yesterday at the lake, the camp was quiet. Most of the campers were confined to their cabins, learning more civilized ways to interact with one another. Dustin didn't mind. He stayed to himself most days. All he needed was the horses, and he was fine. He heard a noise behind him. At the same time, Gretel's ears perked up. Turning, he found Tricia Hanson standing behind him.

"Hi." He said, his voice a higher pitch than normal.

"Hey." She said, looking around the stable. "You spend a lot of time here." She continued.

"I like horses." He explained, leaning against the door to Gretel's stall. She moved slowly toward him.

"We know." Her tone showed the other campers were all aware of the boy that hung out every day in the stables, hardly interacting with the other campers.

"They're easier to get along with than people." He explained. She shrugged her shoulders while coming to stand directly beside him.

"So, who is this?" She asked.

"This is Gretel."

"Like the story book?"

"Yes."

"Doesn't seem fair?"

"What do you mean?"

"You should never have a Gretel without a Hansel."
He smiled, completely loving her analogy.

"I agree." He said, then took a step back and turned
to face the stall next to them, prompting Tricia to extend
her neck, noticing the black horse.

"Meet Hansel." She laughed a little, standing next to
the beam separating the two horses' stalls.

"Well, now it makes sense." She smiled. A look on
her that Dustin never saw up close. Not that anyone got
close to Tricia.

"Would you like to help me brush them?" Dustin
asked suggestively.

"I wouldn't know what to do?"

"I can show you." He noticed her shuffle the ball of
her foot around before shrugging her shoulders again.

"Sure." She answered. Dustin nodded and walked
over to the other side of the stable, grabbing a two-step
stool.

"You'll want to stand on this." He motioned while
placing the stool against the door to Gretel's stall. He
watched as she eagerly and fearlessly stepped onto the
stool. Turning, he lifted his hand palm flat toward Gretel,
who'd retreated to the back of the stall the moment Tricia
approached.

"What does that do?" she asked. He placed his
finger over his lips to silence her. He could almost feel the
annoyance rising inside of her, but she stayed quiet. Gretel
walked over to them a few seconds later, placing her head
on Dustin's palm, and he began to scratch lightly.

"Gretel needs to trust you first. Horses are very
particular and don't come to just anyone." Tricia nodded,
her annoyance at him silencing her, fading away. Dustin

grabbed the brush from the slim wooden shelf on the beam between the two stalls. He placed the brush in Tricia's open hand and assisted her in brushing Gretel.

"Her hair is smooth." Tricia said. She was smiling again, and Dustin liked this version of her, much more than the scowling face she normally displayed.

"It's called her coat." He corrected gently. He didn't want to upset her. He liked this side of Tricia. He could probably guess on one hand how many other campers had the chance to experience her in this way. He also knew if he upset her, her mood might scare Gretel, and he didn't want that.

"Thank you for yesterday." She said, interrupting his thoughts. He looked over at her. She was in mid-stroke brushing Gretel, staring at him almost nervously. He shouldn't have been shocked by her words, but he was sure she wasn't used to thanking anyone.

"It's no problem. I don't like what they did."

"They're jerks." She said, handing him the brush and stepping off the stool.

"Not all boys are like that."

"Except for you and Ethan, I disagree." She was standing a few steps away from him with both her arms folded. Dustin placed the brush back on the shelf and turned to face her. His thoughts had been to console her. Seeing how upset she was by yesterday's events. He wasn't sure where the instinct to reach out and potentially hug her came from. He didn't even make it two steps before he heard.

"There you are?" They both turned to see Tanya walking into the barn. "I have been searching all morning for you. This is the last place I expected you to be. Hey

Dustin." She added a little flirtiness in her voice when acknowledging him.

"Hey, Tanya." She winked at his response, and to his surprise, Tricia came to stand right in front of her with both hands on her hips.

"Stop flirting with him." Tricia almost barked. The shock on Tanya's face was followed by a quick shift in the atmosphere as Tanya then returned the scowling face; he was sure matched Tricia's.

"Staking a claim now, Tricia?" Tanya said, folding her arms. He watched the interaction between the two girls. Not fully sure if he should interrupt them or stay quiet, he chose the latter. Looking at Tricia from behind, he noticed her head was down, and her right heel shuffled back and forth before lifting her head and facing Tanya again.

"What if I am?" Dustin's eyebrows hunched in confusion to Tricia's response. What was she staking a claim to? What was going on? The silence hung in the air for a few seconds, then Tanya threw her head back and laughed, unfolded her arms and raised them in surrender.

"I never thought I'd see this day come." Tricia's stance never changed, as Tanya's now cheery disposition was evident on her face. "Well, I'll just go hang out with Ethan." Tanya turned to leave the barn with an extra pep in her step. "Don't do anything I wouldn't do." she called out with a wink as she left the stables.

"What just happened?" He asked, still unsure of the underlying encounter between the two friends.

"Nothing." Tricia said, turning back to face him. She walked back over to the two-step stool in front of Gretel's stall door. He watched her step up on the stool, grab the brush and look over at him.

"You're just officially my boyfriend."

Chapter Four

Nadia walked into her one-bedroom apartment and slowly closed the door. Still, in her wedding dress, she gently rested the back of her head against it. Married? She was married. And her name wasn't even Nadia Bolton. It was Tricia something. She didn't know how to process what happened today. Slowly stepping away from the door, she headed to her bedroom. Her queen-size bed with her flowery bed cover looked completely inviting after the morning fiasco of a wedding or non-wedding occurrence. She accepted the invitation and plopped face first into her mattress, smelling the vanilla-scented Febreze air freshener. Kicking her leg and muttering into her mattress, she practically expelled the screams she had been holding in. It was all she could do. All she knew to do. The muffled screams eventually turned into sobbing tears, and the constant entanglement of emotions flowed through her. Twelve years, twelve long years of her knowing nothing of her past life. Twelve years of her thinking she was some abandoned child or teen. Twelve years of trying to find out where she belonged, who she belonged with and what to do. Finally turning over, because of her ranting fits of crying making it hard for her to breathe, she laid on her back and stared at her ceiling, allowing her tears to flow. She closed her eyes, and gray eyes appeared in her mind. She quickly reopened her eyes and sat up. No, she wouldn't think about him. He'd plague her mind enough for the last three weeks. She thought she was going crazy to see his gray eyes everywhere she went. After the initial shock and her passing out, she woke up in a small room in the back of the church with her fiancé and so-called husband. She actually had a husband. Could life get any more confusing? She'd been so shocked to see him. She even told him he was rude to her the first time they'd met. She couldn't even look at Kyle. What could she say to him? Kyle's mother and uncle demanded more proof besides a marriage license, and Dustin pulled out an old photo. It wasn't a wedding photo, but a photo of the two of them next to a horse. Kyle practically snatched the photo from her before she could get a full look at it, claiming one photo meant nothing. Dustin stepped toward Kyle with a menacing look, berating him for snatching the photo. Ashiree tried to calm Dustin, Kyle took another step toward Dustin and then Sean, Ashiree's bodyguard, stepped in, and she yelled "ENOUGH" from everyone before storming out of the room. She heard both Dustin and Kyle call her name, but she wasn't listening. She had to get out of there. Kyle caught up to her grabbing her arm to stop her.

"You can't just leave. We have to figure this out."

"You might want to let her go." Dustin stated.

"Stay out of this." Kyle barked at Dustin while still holding her arm. She snatched her arm away from him. She tried to make him understand. She needed time to process, breathe, and figure out what to do next. Thankfully, Dustin had remained quiet and seemed to understand her need to take some time to herself.

Looking down now at her hands in her lap, she wondered how much time she would need. Her entire world shifted today and not in the way she'd thought. Kyle clearly expressed his reservations about her being around Dustin, but how could she not be around him. He was the only person who knew about her past. She might get answers and shine some light on the dark abyss that was her life before she woke up in that medical center. Rising slowly, she headed for her connecting bathroom and turned on the shower. She set the temperature as hot as she could take it, stripped off her wedding dress and allowed herself to find some solace in the shower. Tomorrow. She'd tackle everything tomorrow.

"**Everything** here is running fine. You just worry about getting things handled there in Houston." Dustin was speaking to his housekeeper Ms. Anita. Checking on things at his ranch and the Equestrian. Dustin considered flying back to his ranch in San Antonio, but he knew his foreman and housekeeper could keep things going while he was gone. Anita was almost seventy and was diagnosed with a rare disease that no doctor seemed to cure. She'd spent over twenty-five years trying every experimental drug they could come up with. Finally deciding to give up, she ended up at his Equestrian, attempting to fulfill a few activities on her bucket list. Falling in love with the horses and choosing to spend her remaining moments there, she'd miraculously healed within six months. That was almost a year ago. Being cured left her void of what to do next in her life. His foreman, Harper, suggested he take on a housekeeper. One of the last things he built was the house that now sat on his property. The two-story five-bedroom farmhouse included a wraparound porch and an upper deck off the master bedroom.

"Thanks, Anita. I'll check back with you and Harper in a few days." He ended the call, rubbed his hand on the back of his neck, and walked into the sitting area of Blake Manor. Hearing Ashiree on the phone with Dominic, he assumed his friend wasn't too happy about the fiasco of the wedding he'd just crashed. A maid asked if he wanted a drink, and he requested water as Ashiree joined him in the sitting room.

"I'm guessing Dominic's not too happy." Dustin said. She waved him off as she placed a sleeping Arion in his baby carrier.

"He just wanted to make sure we were okay. He's on his way home."

"Because of what happened?" Dustin asked with a quirked brow.

"No, he's surprising me with my best friend, Chelsea."

"If you know that, then it's not a surprise."

"I'll still act surprised, but Chelsea told me last week. She knows I hate surprises." Dustin shook his head.

"But no more talking about me. What are you going to do about Nadia?"

"She wants time. I can't do anything but give her that. I'm sure she has a lot of questions."

"I'm sure she does. But why didn't you say anything before."

"Honestly, Donnie confirmed my suspicions this morning. Then he told me she was getting married today. I didn't think about anything but getting to the wedding."

"Well, you certainly made it a close call."

"A news chopper was in the area, and I didn't get clearance to land closer to the church." She nodded, then moved to grab something out of her purse on the couch next to her.

"I thought you might want this back. Kyle dropped this when Nadia left the room." She was about to get up to hand it to him, but he moved faster than her.

"You guys look really happy." She said as he took the old picture from her.

"We were only kids back then. Hopeful. Full of dreams and very much in love." Ashiree nodded, but they both heard the front door to the Manor opening, and the butler escorted Donnell into the sitting room before she could respond.

"Hi, Donnie." Dustin watched as Donnell greeted Ashiree by leaning down to kiss her cheek.

"It's good to see you, Ashiree. And thank you for your help." Donnell said. He walked over to Dustin, who stood to greet him with a hug.

"Thanks for today, Donnie."

"I'm not too sure you'll thank me when I tell you what I've stumbled upon." Dustin quirked a brow as Donnell looked over to Ashiree.

"Do you mind if we use the conference room to talk?"

"Of course not. Knock yourself out. I'll just take Arion to the nursery. Oh, and Donnie, there are some double fudge chocolate chip cookies in the kitchen with your name written on them." She said, smiling sweetly.

"You keep spoiling me with sweets, and Dominic's going to get jealous." She waved her hand dismissively as she picked Arion up.

"We compromised on that. As long as I only make brownies for him, he will concede all other sweets to you." Dustin watched curiously between the two of them as they shared a laugh. As Ashiree retreated with Arion in her arms, he and Donnell entered the conference room.

"What's with you and Ashiree with the sweets?" Dustin asked as he closed the door, and Donnell pulled his laptop out of his bag.

"That woman can bake her butt off, but she and Dominic got into a fuss when he suggested she stay home and not work her last few weeks being pregnant. Ashiree basically bribed me with cookies to change the code on the colonial so that Dom couldn't get in." Donnell said with a chuckle. Dustin knew Donnell was referring to the Four-bedroom colonial house behind Blake Manor. A house Dominic's father had built for his mother.

"And you did it?" Dustin asked, slightly astound.

"It was all in good fun." He responded with a light shrug as he turned his laptop on. "What I didn't suspect was Dominic acting like he was some sort of spiderman and climbing up the side of the house. It was really hard for me and Sean to explain to the security company that all the alarms were going off because one spouse wanted to lock the other out of the house." Dustin just shook his head at how ridiculous it sounded until he realized Tricia might have done the same thing. That thought prompted him to ask Donnell about what he found.

"So, what did you find out that made you drive all the way over?"

"Just this." Donnell said as he turned his laptop towards Dustin, displaying an old article. Dustin looked at the two couples displayed in the picture. One couple he recognized immediately, the other he did not. Squinting his eyes, he said.

"Ok, I know these are Tricia's parents, but who is the other couple?" he asked, pointing to the right side of the picture. Donnell told him, and Dustin's eyebrows shot up in surprise.

"They know each other?" Dustin asked.

"They do and have for quite some time." Donnell responded while indicating the date of the article. With that knowledge, Dustin took a seat at the conference table, and Donnell did too.

"Do you think they know she's alive?" Dustin asked.

"It would be surprising if they didn't."

"Why keep it a secret?"

"I don't know. I'm still looking into some things. But Ashiree thought it would be a good idea for me to talk to Nadia about who she was."

"Do you not agree?"

"I'm fine with telling her whatever she wants to know. But this..." he said, pointing to the article. "...I'm not too sure I want to spring on her. I wanted your opinion. You know more about her relationship with her parents than I would. Should I tell her?" Donnell asked. Dustin rubbed the back of his neck. Tricia never had the best relationship with her parents, and Nadia had no clue of anything of her past.

"I wouldn't just yet. Not until you find out why they kept this a secret." Donnell nodded at Dustin's response.

"I'll keep digging then. But I'm quite sure none of us will like what I find. This reeks of a major mess."

"You have no idea." Dustin said, dreading what might lie underneath what had been going on the last twelve years.

Dustin at sixteen:

"I can't believe they're actually coming this year." Tricia complained.

"They're your parents Tricia." Dustin sat next to Ethan on a bench log, watching Tricia pace in front of the lake as Tanya tried to calm her down. Tomorrow was Parents' Day at the camp. He knew his father could not make it this year. The last few months, he'd been getting sick. Then in a few days, he'd feel better only to fall sick again a week later.

"They're only coming because of Dustin." She practically shouted as she extended her hand in reference to him but focused on Tanya.

"You've never had a boyfriend, Tricia, and I'm sure you've been tight-lipped about it."

"Well, you and Ethan are together. I don't see your parents coming tomorrow."

"Please, as long as I don't get arrested or come home pregnant, my parents couldn't care less."

"You're so lucky." Tricia responded annoyingly and folded her arms in frustration. Tanya threw her hands up in surrender and walked over to him and Ethan.

"You're up, Dustin. I can't get through to her. Ethan, let's go get an ice cream cone." He didn't watch Ethan and Tanya walk away. His focus was on Tricia. Arms still folded, back stiff, she was looking out toward the lake. He walked over to stand beside her.

"Is them coming here really that bad?"

"They're coming to break us up." She answered, still looking out at the water.

"They can't break us up, Tricia."

"You don't know them, Dustin." She stated firmly, finally looking over at him.

"Then I'll meet them and get to know them."

"I'd rather you didn't." Dustin did his best not to flinch at her answer.

"Are you ashamed of me?" He asked hesitantly. It was the first time he ever questioned if she might have an issue with him being mixed-raced.

"No. I'm ashamed of them." She answered, reassuring him. He put his arm around her and kissed her temple.

"It will all work out then. Don't worry so much about it." He watched as she bowed her head and shuffled her right foot on her heel before speaking.

"They're not coming alone." She answered softly.

"What do you mean?" She slowly looked up at him.

"My mom's old college friend is coming and bringing her son. A suitable boyfriend, as they call it."

"They're just going to throw some boy at you?"

"They see it as doing what's best for me."

"And they're bringing him here to sort of size up the competition." He stated more than questioned. He was beginning to understand her annoyance with her parents.

"Most likely, and that's why I don't want you to meet them. If they know nothing about us, they can't use anything against you and try to break us up." He kept his arm around her but looked back out in the water himself. He didn't like feeling as though he needed to hide. Like he was some blemish that no one wanted to see. He'd spent most of his childhood that way. The son of a wealthy real-estate mogul that no one knew about. The illegitimate child, the secret.

"Please, Dusty?" He looked back down at her. Connecting his gray eyes to her brown ones and seeing the true stress in them. He loved this girl. Probably since the first moment, he saw her throw Ethan over her shoulder like a sack of potatoes. He needed to trust her judgment when it came to her parents. Even Ethan and Tanya previously stated their ploys to control Tricia's life. He wanted to help, but sometimes trying to help only made things worse. Love was about trust and sacrifice. His mother had told him that, and he loved Tricia more than he ever thought he could love another person.

"I won't meet them if you don't want me to." He saw the biggest relief in her eyes, followed by her leaning up to kiss him, thank you, and hugging him as if holding on for dear life. He wrapped his arms around her just as tightly and prayed his decision to trust her was the right one.

Chapter Five

Nadia sat in her office at Gateway Pharmaceuticals and tried to focus on her work. Technically she was supposed to be returning from her honeymoon today. Kyle had been calling her non-stop. With the media constantly reporting the outcome of their wedding, his poll numbers were dropping, and his political image was being tarnished. She wasn't sure what he expected her to do. There was no way she could have predicted she had a husband or that he would crash her wedding. Speaking of her so-called husband, she had not heard from him. She'd been brave enough to ask Ashiree about him a couple of days ago and discovered he'd been a guest at Blake Manor for the last week. Dustin was friends with Ashiree's husband, her CEO, Dominic Blake. She would never be so bold as to ask Mr. Blake himself about Dustin. He wasn't intimidating or rude. Dominic Blake was a nice man, a complete gentleman and treated his wife like a queen. She'd only seen him lose his temper once. Last year, Dominic was named CEO instead of her former, and now deceased, CFO Brian Fallon. In that same meeting, while Dominic was introducing himself to the staff, his encounter with Ashiree caused her to throw up on him before passing out in front of everyone. At the time, Brian demanded Ashiree be fired from Gateway. Nadia could shamefully admit initially, she had agreed with Brian. It was a completely embarrassing situation to happen to their newly appointed CEO. Dominic stood almost toe-to-toe with Brian expressing why firing Ashiree was not taking place. After hearing Dominic's reasonings and knowing that a mistake or incident of that nature should not cause staff members to lose their jobs, she had to agree. Others could argue that he had a personal interest in Ashiree, and that's why he fought for her to stay employed, but as she'd watched him interact with the staff and board members, she knew that was his character. Sitting back and rubbing her eyes, unable to focus, she heard a knock on her office door.

"Come in." She called.

"Hey." Ashiree said, standing in her doorway.

"Hi! What are you doing here? I thought you were still on maternity leave."

"Oh, I am. Dominic is showing Arion around to everyone in the lab." Nadia chuckled. Dominic was a true papa bear.

"I think that's really sweet." Nadia admitted.

"He's a sweet guy for sure, but it allowed me to come to see and check on you."

"Sure, have a seat." Ashiree walked into her office, closed the door, and took a seat in the chair in front of her cherry wood desk.

"So, how are you?"

"As good as can be expected. I honestly don't know how I'm supposed to feel." Nadia said, shrugging her shoulders.

"I get that. I didn't know how to feel either after finding out my father is alive, and I have three younger siblings."

"Really?"

"Yup, Donnie told me on Christmas morning."

"Who's Donnie?" Nadia asked.

"Donnell. Another friend of Dominic's. He's a tech genius, but I think he works secretly for the government in some capacity. Anyway, he's the one who confirmed who you were to Dustin." Nadia nodded, feeling as though she understood Ashiree's visit.

"He has some information for me, doesn't he." Ashiree nodded, not even hiding the agenda behind her visit.

"How am I supposed to get this information? Does he want to meet me?"

"He does. We thought the Manor would be neutral ground, so you wouldn't have to meet him alone if you didn't want to."

"Will Dustin be there?" She wasn't sure why seeing him scared her. Especially knowing that he knew answers about her and her past that even this Donnell guy couldn't find out.

"He doesn't have to be. Dustin is a pretty patient guy. He's not trying to pressure you to talk to him about anything until you're ready." She nodded, thinking that was the opposite of how Kyle felt. Then immediately stopped her thoughts. She didn't want to compare Kyle to Dustin. No one knew the best way to handle this situation.

"Can I ask you a question?" Nadia asked, shifting uneasily in her chair.

"Sure?" Ashiree answered.

"What would you do?" Nadia watched Ashiree bite her lip, thinking about how to answer.

"When I had my suspicions about Ashden being my brother, I went back and forth on whether I should investigate, taking a chance on finding out I wasn't alone in the world. I could have been let down or disappointed. I mean, I have my best friend Chelsea, and me and Dominic secretly married, but it is nothing like having your own family. So, I basically jumped at the opportunity, which got slightly interrupted by me being kidnapped." She said with a slight laugh. Nadia couldn't help but laugh with her. The kidnapping was far from laughable, but to move on from something like that, was a blessing.

"Anyway. I haven't spent much time with my dad or my siblings. His wife isn't too fond of some nameless child coming out of nowhere and disrupting her family."

"That sounds pretty insensitive." Nadia said. Ashiree shrugged and continued.

"My point is, either way, there will be good and bad in finding out about your past, what you've lost or missed out on. I still haven't found my mother, and my father honestly doesn't remember most of the women in the 'sowing his royal oats' stage of his life. It's not pretty, and I'm sure we have ways to go. But the idea of not knowing, the fear of never finding out, is gone, and I don't regret it. If we never become a happy-go-lucky family, I'll never regret finding them." Nadia nodded in understanding and appreciated Ashiree's honesty. She didn't want to fear never finding out her past, how she ended up in a medical center, losing her memory and why everyone thought she was dead. A slight knock on the door captured her and Ashiree's attention.

"Come in." Nadia answered.

"Sorry, I hope I'm not interrupting." Nadia and Ashiree looked over as the new assistant to the CFO was standing in the doorway.

"Not at all, Camille." Nadia said, waving her hand to invite her over.

"How can I help you?" Camille walked over to stand by the side of Nadia's desk.

"Actually, I'm here for Mrs. Blake." She shifted her stance to face Ashiree. "Mr. Blake is requesting your assistance. Apparently, there is an issue with him retrieving little Arion from the clutches of Ms. Sands. His words, not mine." Ashiree giggled.

"Oh lord. I told Dominic not to go to the marketing area without me. Let me go save my child." Ashiree stood. "Nadia, call me or text later. I'll get you Donnie's contact information, and you can go from there."

"Thanks, Ashiree." Ashiree said her goodbyes and quickly left the office.

"They really are a cute couple." Camille stated.

"Yes, they are." Nadia agreed.

"Are you alright?" Camille asked. Nadia nodded. Several of the employees and staff at Gateway were aware of the fiasco that was her wedding, and most seemed genuine in their concern over how she was handling it.

"As good as can be." she replied. It was her standard answer over the last week. And honestly, it was the truth. She was still wrapping her mind around it all.

"I was going to head to the staff lounge for some tea. Would you like a cup?" Nadia smiled at Camille's thoughtfulness. While some like coffee as their choice of caffeine, Nadia preferred tea, and a cup of tea sounded heavenly right now.

"Yes, I wouldn't mind a cup. Thank you, Camille."

Dustin sat back in a lounge chair in the game room at Blake Manor. He watched as Dillon and Dexter played pool while Dominic held a sleeping Arion on his lap, and Darwin showed Kaley how to play a game on the Xbox. Damien stood off to the side of the pool table.

"Is anyone else curious how we've known Dustin for over ten years and didn't know he was married?" Dillon asked.

"Technically, he thought he was a widow." Dexter said, aiming his cue for the next shot.

"Does that even matter?" Darwin chimed in, still focused on playing the game with Kaley.

"I still would like to know." Damien stated.

"So would I." Dominic added. Dustin watched as Dillon and Dexter stood with their pool sticks upright beside them and faced him. He breathed a sigh before he spoke.

"I met Tricia, or Nadia, when I was twelve years old." It still felt weird thinking of her as Nadia. "We ended up attending the same summer camp. I went every summer for six years. I saw her name carved in my bunk on my first day there. It was strange, considering the guys and girls were in separate cabins and on different sides of the camp. I got to meet her, or rather see her, in action that first day.

"See her in action?" Dominic asked. Dustin nodded.

"Yes, on the first day of camp, she was wrestling with a boy almost twice her size and tossed him over her shoulder like he was nothing."

"Tomboy?" Dexter asked.

"The biggest. But after a couple of years, she started developing like most girls and had to tone some things down. She didn't by much, but a few boys decided to play a prank on her and snatch the top part of her bikini off a couple of summers after that. I ended up decking one of them."

"Played the whole knight in shining armor thing, huh?" Dillon asked, smiling.

"Not really. He was a jerk that used to bully me. with Matthew." Heads nodded, knowing Dustin didn't have the best relationship with his older brothers.

"Besides, Tricia was probably mad I got the first hit. Long story short, she practically declared me her boyfriend the next day, and we were pretty much inseparable after that. We got married after we both turned eighteen.

"I swear you and Dom are more alike than I thought." Damien stated.

"Why didn't you ever say anything?" Dominic asked. Dustin took another deep breath.

"I didn't know what to say. How do you tell people your wife died? When's a good time to bring that up in conversation? Honestly, I wanted to forget it. The accident, all of it. In a three-year span, I lost my mom, my wife, and my dad. I only went to college because Tricia wanted me to. Well, she wanted us to. The first year I was like a zombie. I had you guys the next few years, which was great, considering my dad passed and Matthew and Jacob had me in and out of court over the real estate business. I have no idea why he left it to me. Honestly, I wanted to give the whole thing up, but the property outside of San Antonio was perfect. It would have been Tricia's dream to have a plot of land that size. It was like I could have a piece of her with me and start building her dream and mine on it."

"You couldn't negotiate for just the land in San Antonio?" Dexter asked.

"Matthew and Jacob both were selfish, and they didn't want me to have any of it. But my dad made it very clear it was all mine in his will. If I didn't want it, he had partners to divide up the business and properties and give it to them. So, it was all or nothing. I wasn't going to give up the property in San Antonio, so I accepted it, all of it. By the time everything settled, we had graduated, and I left to start the ranch."

"You still could have said something, Dustin. Clearly, you were hurt." Dillon stated.

"What could I do? She was gone. My mom was gone. I just coped the best I could."

"I get that." Darwin said.

"So do I." Dominic added. Dustin nodded slowly. Both Dominic and Darwin had lost their moms, so he knew they understood his pain.

"So, what do you plan to do now?" Dexter asked.

"Honestly, Dexter, I don't know. My wife is still gone. Nadia has no memory of me or Tricia or the life we planned to share together."

"Are you going to fight for her anyway?" Darwin asked.

"I'm not sure if she'd want me to. Once she finds out everything, whether she ever remembers, she might not choose me. She still has a fiancé."

"What ever happened to true love conquers all?" Damien stated.

"Look at Damien, being all romantic." Dillon said, astonished.

"I'm as shocked as you are." Dexter added.

"Screw the both of you." Damien countered.

"Well, you do have the cards in your favor." Dominic interrupted, picking up Arion as he began to fuss.

"How do you mean?" Dustin asked.

"You're already married to her. You got her to fall in love with you once. You can do it again."

Dustin at sixteen:

"This is the last time I let you and Tanya talk me into this." Dustin smiled, listening to Tricia rant and complain about her dress as they walked over to the main cabin hall. The camp decided this year to add a dance before the end of the summer. While every other girl was excited and heavy with anticipation, Tricia was unimpressed and uninterested. They'd been a couple for over a year now. After Tricia's bold declaration of him as her boyfriend, they practically have been inseparable the rest of the summer. They exchanged numbers and email addresses and spent every moment outside of school talking to each other. Tricia's parents were extremely strict and only allowed her two hours on the phone a day, which is when email came into play. She could claim to be doing homework while talking to him in a private chat room. His dad didn't care how much time he spent on the phone, as long as he excelled in his studies, kept his status on the wrestling team and did not visit the dean's office as much as his brothers did. Things were slightly different at home now that Matthew and Jacob were both in college. Jacob and their dad had a big falling out, and he didn't come home for the holidays. Although he tried to play it off, Dustin knew it bothered his dad. Matthew spent the entire holiday partying with old friends, bringing them by the house to get plastered drunk off their dad's whiskey bar. Dustin stayed to himself in his room. When he wasn't talking or chatting with Tricia, he took apart old VCRs, television tubes, and computers, then put them back together. He wasn't sure why it fascinated him, but it did. His dad caught him one day, and Dustin thought he would be furious, but he just chuckled and said, "What are you, a modern-day MacGyver?" Dustin frowned in confusion, not understanding the reference. His dad, realizing he didn't know what he meant, introduced him to the 1985 series by playing recorded episodes on one of the VCRs he hadn't taken apart. He loved it. The man could make a bomb out of anything. Not that Dustin wanted to make a bomb, but he did like the thought process it took to do so.

"I never thought Dustin could convince you to wear a dress. You look so pretty." Tanya exclaimed, interrupting his thoughts and complementing Tricia. He had to agree with Tanya. Tricia looked pretty in her burgundy spaghetti strap dress that hit just above her knees. Tanya was dressed in a baby blue sundress with matching earrings.

"He's just lucky I like him enough to come to this." Tricia answered dryly. Dustin smiled, placing a kiss on her temple. He was very much aware if he hadn't asked her to go, she wouldn't have given the dance a fleeting thought.

"I just can't understand why you're not excited about this. It's the camp's first dance." Tanya excitedly said. Tricia didn't crack a smile.

"Well, I'm excited." The threesome turned to see Ethan walking up dressed in a khaki shirt and some shorts.

"Really, Ethan?" Tanya complained.

"What?" He asked, both hands out as he looked over his attire.

"Shorts to a dance?" She asked with her hands on her hips.

"Did you expect a suit?" She rolled her eyes, grabbed his hand, and headed into the dance hall. It wasn't too much longer after Tricia's bold declaration of claiming him that Tanya and Ethan became an item. The four of them got along pretty well. Ethan, like him, was far from the little boy he saw Tricia throw over her shoulder his first year at camp. He was almost as tall as Dustin but broad-built. Dustin wasn't surprised when Ethan told him he'd made the varsity football team. It was all Ethan talked about, Tanya and football. They found a table closest to the back. All the tables and chairs circled around in what was now designated as the dance floor. Normally it was their mess hall for meals. A few of the boys gave a chin up to him and Ethan, but most stared the minute they saw Tricia. Dustin was pretty sure none of them expected to see her show up and definitely not in a dress. Tanya and Ethan headed over to the punch and dessert table as he and Tricia took a seat.

"Everyone is staring at me." Tricia said arms folded, resting back in her chair.

"You're beautiful. What do you expect?" He thought she would roll her eyes at him like she normally did when he paid her a compliment. Instead, she was looking at her boots, shuffling her foot left and right.

"I wish you wouldn't say that."

"Why not?"

"Because it is not true. I'm just...okay." He leaned over, almost resting his head on her folded arms, knowing her eyes would connect with his.

"You're more than okay. You just don't flaunt it, which I happen to like about you. But clearly, you could see everyone's shock when you walked in. You're beautiful, Tricia...and before you try to argue that fact with me, understand you can't change what I see." He lifted his head and kissed her cheek, receiving a smile from her he knew she was trying to fight. She conceded, unfolding her arms and placing them on his shoulders. Leaning her head against his, he took in her scent. It was subtle but sweet, like vanilla. He loved moments like this. When her guard was slightly down, she relaxed and just enjoyed the moment. Over the last year of their dating, he began to understand the reason behind Tricia's tough exterior. Her parents were hard on her, always demanding perfection, and any signs of weakness was unacceptable.

"Dance with me." He said. She tensed, lifted her head, connecting her eyes with his.

"I don't know how to dance, Dusty." He felt her shifting her foot under the table.

"I'll show you." He scooted back and stood, extending his hand to her.

"Come on, Trixie." She rolled her eyes, took his hand, and stood.

"I don't know why you call me that. I'm not as bad as that little girl." She huffed, knowing he referred to the little girl from the movie 'Problem Child 2'.

"No, you're definitely worse." He teased while kissing her temple. She playfully swatted at him as they made their way to the dance floor. Taking her in his arms, he heard a song play in the background that he knew described the love he had only for her. Love stronger than anything he'd ever known, love that would never waver, love that was endless.

Chapter Six

Nadia took her seat with Fiona and Margery as they finally entered the Breakfast Klub. The line was wrapped around the building to get in, but the wait was worth it, and the food was excellent.

"So, how are you?" Fiona asked, adding sugar to her coffee. How was she? That was a loaded question. And one she wasn't sure how to answer.

"I'm taking it all in?" She answered honestly.

"Have you spoken to Kyle?"

"A little. He isn't too happy about how everything's been going."

"Can you blame him?" Margery said.

"Yes, she can blame him." Fiona interrupted. "She just found out she has a husband, a significant key to her past if you ask me."

"So, you think she should just give up on her relationship with Kyle?" Margery said.

"I think it's safe to say that relationship is on hold."

"You two realize you can continue this conversation without me?" Nadia said.

"Oh! Nadia. I'm sorry. We get carried away sometimes." Fiona said, reaching her hand out to pat Nadia on the arm.

"It's fine." Nadia assured her.

"Soooo, have you spent any time with this new husband of yours?" Margery asked.

"I haven't been focused on the new husband yet, whose name is Dustin, by the way. Ashiree Blake helped me get in contact with a guy who has some information on who I used to be." Nadia said, feeling nervous at the thought.

"Well, I think that's amazing." Fiona replied. The waitress brought over their food, and Nadia sighed at the omelet. The first bite was pure heaven.

"So back to this, Dustin. Does he have a last name?" Margery asked.

"Shaw. Dustin Shaw." Nadia answered.

"Your husband is Dustin Shaw?" Nadia and Fiona whipped their heads towards Margery at the sound of her fork hitting on the table.

"Have you heard of him?" Nadia asked curiously.

"Yes, but most people haven't. I only know about him because my dad's firm handled his brother's lawsuit." Margery answered.

"Lawsuit? What Lawsuit?" Fiona asked before Nadia could. Margery leaned into the center of the table and kept her voice low.

"My dad's firm handles a lot of cases with clients dealing with real-estate. The only reason I remember this particular case is because it lasted what seemed forever, and my dad's firm lost. He doesn't lose many cases, hardly any actually, so this one still stings. Anyway, this mega real estate guru guy dies and leaves his entire real-estate fortune and empire to his illegitimate son. Naturally, his two older sons contested the will and fought the youngest for it. I've never seen my dad so stressed. It almost put a strain on my parents' marriage. I was working for my dad one weekend when a man named Matthew Shaw showed up practically threatening my dad if he didn't win this case. He kept shouting at him about how some half-breed that he'd only known a few years couldn't come in and steal what was his. My dad tried to explain the will was ironclad, and there was nothing he could do unless they gave up some property in San Antonio, which this Matthew guy was unwilling to do. So, the judge ruled in favor of the will, bequeathing everything to a young man named Dustin Shaw." She finished and leaned back in her chair.

"And you think Nadia's husband is the same Dustin Shaw?"

"Yes."

"What makes you so sure?" Nadia asked.

"Well, for one, we know he's white or mixed from what Matthew said."

"And for two?" Fiona asked.

"His connection to Dominic Blake."

"They're both rich, and they could easily run in the same circles." Fiona stated.

"True, but I know for a fact that Dustin Shaw was connected to the Blakes before the lawsuit."

"How?" Both Nadia and Fiona asked simultaneously.

"Because my dad's firm had to face the one man on the opposing counsel that my dad knew he couldn't win against." Margery said, taking a sip of her mimosa.

"Who?" They both asked.

"Randall Davison, legal counsel to the Blake family and Blake Enterprises."

Dustin rubbed his neck as he entered his guestroom in Blake Manor. It was another Thursday night, and dinner at Blake Manor was becoming a sort of tradition. Normally he would make it once or twice a month, depending on what was going on at the ranch. However, staying in Houston and sorting things out with Nadia, he became a regular at every nightly dinner. The ranch took up so much of his time but being around his friends seemed to satisfy a longing in his heart that he hadn't been aware was there. The attendees on Thursday nights varied depending on everyone's schedule. Damien was not in attendance because of the Houston baseball team playing in San Diego. Dustin happily sat back and watched. He wasn't a big talker and only engaged in the conversation when needed. Both Dominic and Darwin seem to slip so easily into the role of father, and it gave him a new light on just how much he missed getting together. Of course, he hadn't completely been a rogue or thrown himself into seclusion as Darwin had, but he had been absent for many events that occurred in his friends' lives. Damien's draft into the MLB, he'd missed. Dillon taking over his uncle's bar, he'd missed. Dexter launching his Dex-It brand, he'd missed. It was something that plagued his mind, and he'd opened up to Harper, his foreman, about it a year ago. He'd just returned from the funeral of Donald Blake, Dominic's grandfather, and knew the weight and toll that Dominic was experiencing. He was glad he attended and made a vow to be there more for his friends shortly after. He didn't have to be at the ranch twenty-four hours a day. He had a full staff and plenty of capable employees to keep things going while he was gone. It allowed him to attend Dominic's private wedding, the birth of his first child and ultimately the baby shower that led him into the situation he was in now. Nadia. She'd been working for Gateway Pharmaceuticals for the last three years. Her role as the Human Resource manager placed her in consistent interaction with Dominic, and she'd formed some sort of friendship with Ashiree. He didn't know how close they were outside of them working together. Ashiree was still new to living in Houston, as she had moved from Boston last year, after being hired at Gateway. However, it seemed some cosmic forces were working in his favor to bring the two of them together, or at least he hoped they were. He hadn't spoken to Nadia. Not that he'd gotten her phone number to do so if he could. He was giving her space. Trying to be as understanding as possible of the situation they were in. Ashiree mentioned at dinner tonight that she reached out to Nadia, and she'd agreed to meet with Donnell. Hopefully, talking with Donnell first would open her up to know more about him and eventually their relationship.

Dustin age Seventeen:

Dustin walked with Tricia as they trotted with Gretel along the bank of the lake.

"I can't believe Brett let that big stallion impregnate my favorite girl."

"His name is Dozer, and it's called breeding."

"Don't be such a smart aleck, Dusty. We, women, do all the real work, don't we, Gretel?" She slightly nudged the reins so she could nuzzle Gretel's side with her face. Gretel seemed to know exactly what Tricia said as she neighed in response. Dustin loved watching the interaction between Gretel and Tricia. Gone was the girl slightly uncomfortable around horses. She was a norm now. Brett let her into the barn to help with the horses. Sometimes she'd even beat him there in the morning. She never mucked the stalls, but she'd talk with him while he did, and that was fine with him. They stopped and took a seat by the bank of the lake. Gretel leaned down, taking a drink, and Tricia stroked her side.

"Have you ever heard of horse healing.?" She asked him, looking out over the lake.

"Horse healing? No. Why do you ask?"

"I was doing some searching online. And found an equine therapy farm."

"Like a horse hospital."

"No, it's for people. Horses have special healing powers." She declared, looking over at him with a smile. He smiled back, loving this side of her, vulnerable, smart, subtle. Not that he was complaining. He liked her sassy, no crap-taking, grab men by the balls side too. She was a force to be reckoned with, and Dustin found himself more in love with her no matter how she was.

"I can agree. I think horses might have special powers, especially Gretel here. Like how her powers changed you to be so soft and sweet." She playfully punched him, and he laughed.

"Don't think for one second I've lost my ability to beat you up. No matter how tall or muscular you continue to get." Dustin flexed his muscles.

"You don't think I can take you on?" He asked playfully, loving the fire rising in her eyes. There was no way she could ever beat him, but he'd never fight back, so she'd always win.

"Not a chance, Dusty Gray." She playfully nudged him.

"Tell me again how you came up with that nickname?" Dustin asked, knowing she'd been trying to come up with a nickname for him since last summer when he began calling her Trixie.

"Well, Dusty was easy, but so many people call you Dusty, so then I thought Dusty Blue, kind of like Misty Blue, the song, but your eyes are gray, not blue, so Dusty Gray it is." She shrugged her shoulders as if her explanation made perfect sense to him. He honestly hadn't cared what she called him.

"I love how that mind of yours works." He leaned over, kissed her temple, and felt her tense slightly.

"I wish my parents did." She said, looking down and playing absentmindedly with a few pebbles on the bank.

"They still want you to be a surgeon?" She nodded but didn't look up.

"I stupidly told them about the horse healing farm, thinking at least they might be happy I wanted to be a doctor of some sort. Of course, my mom went ballistic, and my dad basically shut down any future conversation about it." He placed his arm around her to comfort her. She didn't immediately lean into him, but after a few seconds, she took a deep breath and sunk into his side.

"Maybe they'll come around."

"I doubt they ever will."

"It's your life, Trixie. If they won't listen, then tell me. I'll support you." She looked up at him with a sly smile.

"So, If I told you I wanted a horse healing farm with a dozen kids in the middle of nowhere, you'd support me?" He chuckled at her exaggeration of the life she wanted.

"Hey. The last time I checked, Tricia Hanson was unstoppable, so if you want a horse healing farm with a ton of kids in the middle of nowhere. I think that's exactly what you should have." She leaned up and kissed him, loving the response he gave her. He meant every word. Placing her arms around him as he pulled her tighter, they listened to the sounds of the camp in the background, heard the rustling of the wind against the lake and the birds chirping in a tree not too far away.

"Dusty Gray."

"Yes, Trixie."

"I want a helicopter too." He looked down at her with a frown.

"A helicopter?" Dustin questioned.

"Yes, if I'm in the middle of nowhere. I could get anywhere faster than a car." He kissed the top of her head again, slightly chuckling.

"I think a helicopter would be cool." Dustin said, completely honest in his answer. It was far-fetched, but Tricia never limited herself in dreaming. Sometimes he wished he had that ability. To dream beyond the norm, to see the world with endless possibilities.

"It would be. I mean, if you can't get there by horseback or helicopter, then you just wouldn't go."

"So, a horse healing farm, a bunch of kids and a helicopter?" He asked in a confirming voice."

"Yup, the perfect life." She said, snuggling closer into him.

"Yeah, Trixie, the perfect life." He could feel the smile on her face against his side and knew if he ever got the chance, he'd give her all of it.

Chapter Seven

Nadia sat in the sitting room of Blake Manor, processing all the information Donnell discovered about her past. Most of it was pretty basic, like her full name, date of birth, her age, her parents, a few hobbies and that she had married Dustin Shaw at eighteen. That thought seemed so far-fetched from the woman she was today, but with her memory loss, she didn't know what things would have seemed normal when she'd been Tricia Hanson. Her parents were alive, which she was pleased to know. They were currently traveling around Europe, and Donnell was working on getting in contact with them. The hardest thing to listen to was the details of her accident, where she was presumed dead. Her car had practically been incinerated, and the body discovered in it obviously was not her. When Donnell researched how she'd ended up at the medical center, a few miles away from the accident, it was concluded that she had somehow ejected from her car, flown over the freeway awning, and ended up in a small riverbank. It explained why she was not taken to the hospital with the other victims from the accident.

A door opened from a hallway not too far from the sitting area, and Nadia noticed her boss and, well, her husband, walking in. Mr. Blake was carrying his son on his shoulder and greeted her. Dustin walked right over to where she sat with Donnell.

"Are you alright?" Dustin asked. She nodded.

"It's a lot to process." She said nervously. The way he looked at her made her feel anxious. There were so many things she wanted to know, but she was a little scared to ask and fearful of what she might also discover.

"Are you thirsty? We could get you something to drink?" Dominic offered.

"No, thank you. I probably should head out. Is Ashiree here?" She asked and noticed Dominic looking over at Dustin before answering her.

"They're not back yet from shopping." She nodded. When she first arrived to speak with Donnell, Ashiree and Dominic's cousin Shannon were heading out to do some shopping, Ashiree was kind enough to ask her if she wanted her to stay, but Nadia assured her she would be fine.

"Let's hope anything is left in the Galleria when they are through." She heard another man say as he entered the sitting area. He bee-lined straight for Dominic, holding his arms out to take baby Arion. Nadia squinted her eyes and was sure she recognized him.

"Ashiree's not that big on shopping." Dominic said, seeming reluctant to want to hand his son over to the other man.

"Shannon is." The man answered jokingly as he took the baby from Dominic. Propping the baby up, he caught sight of her. "No one told me we had company."

"This is Nadia Bolton." Donnell said before anyone else could speak.

"Ah, the long-lost wife." He said, walking over with Arion to greet her.

"Damien Storm." He announced, extending his hand. Now she placed the face with the name. Of course, she'd recognize him. He was the number one-hitter for the Houston baseball team.

"Nice to meet you." She said, accepting his hand.

"The pleasure is all mine." He said with a wink. Slowly releasing her hand, Arion decided at that moment to spit up all over his shirt.

"Aww, come on, buddy." Damien exclaimed. Now holding Arion away from him.

"Serves you right," Dustin said dryly.

"What? You're supposed to flirt with a pretty girl." He said, winking at Nadia again. She shook her head as Dominic walked over to retrieve his son.

"Like mother, like son." He said, walking away with Damien, as Nadia did her best not to laugh. She wondered if Dominic referred to Ashiree throwing up on him in the conference room last year.

"Nadia." Dustin's low voice instantly brought her eyes to his. Those gray eyes, she could get lost in them.

"Yes?" She answered.

"Will you take a walk with me?" She looked over at Donnell, who nodded his encouragement. Nadia stood slowly, and Dustin extended his hand to assist her. She accepted it, and he led her out of the sitting room onto the deck. Stepping down the cobblestone stairs and onto the walkway, she took in the scene behind Blake Manor. Trees encompassed the estate, giving it a fortress-like image. He led her toward the gardens, and she marveled at the beautiful flowers and plants along the trail that led to a greenhouse. She noticed a vegetable garden and assumed Ashiree was growing her own vegetables. Shortly after approaching the greenhouse, she noticed tall bushes, almost as if they were walls.

"What is that?" Nadia questioned.

"It's a Labyrinth." Dustin answered.

"A what?"

"A Labyrinth, better known as a garden maze."

"I've never heard of it." Then she stopped and looked at Dustin. "Have I heard of it?" She asked him. He looked at her and slightly laughed.

"Honestly, I don't know." He said with a smirk.

"Oh. Sorry." She let go of his hand, realizing she still held it. "I don't know how to do this." She admitted. It felt strange. She didn't know how she was supposed to feel. She knew they'd met as young kids, according to Donnell. But how much had she really shared? Was she the type of woman or girl to tell him all her secrets? Had she known all of his? It was so much that she didn't know where to begin.

"I don't either." She heard him say honestly. It eased her nerves a little.

"We're practically strangers. I mean, I don't know you, but you know me." She responded. He shook his head.

"I know Tricia or knew her. You haven't been Tricia in twelve years. I hope to get the chance to know Nadia. That's if you're willing. You have a different life now, a career… a fiancé." At the mention of Kyle, her heart constricted. She could tell that wasn't easy for him to say, and she felt awful. How had she woven herself into this web? She didn't want to hurt Kyle, But how could she not? She was married to another man. She didn't want to hurt Dustin either.

"I don't want to hurt you, either of you." She admitted, feeling the anxiety swelling up inside of her. This could turn out so bad, and it would be all her fault. She should have tried harder to discover who she'd been. Maybe posted flyers or an ad. She could have even searched ancestry.com. She had done none of that. She'd preferred to believe she was alone in the world and assumed, had she meant something to anyone, they would have found her. It never occurred to her that her family would have thought she wasn't alive. She just tried to live with the cards life dealt her.

"Hey." Dustin said calmly. He placed his hand on her chin and stroked it with his thumb. Her eyes connected with his. "Don't try to figure this all out right now. You want to find out who you are, or were, right?" She nodded, trying to blink back the tears that threatened to escape her eyes. "We'll start there. You can ask me anything. I'll always be truthful with you, okay?"

"Okay." She answered after taking a deep breath. It seemed so easy for him to calm her nerves, and she wondered for just a second if it was something he'd done before.

"Are you interested in taking a ride with me?" She was surprised by his invitation and liked the idea of getting a way for a moment.

"Sure." She answered. She started to turn and walk back toward the Manor. His hand reached out to stop her.

"Not that way." He said, slightly nudging her to follow him. She quirked a brow as they passed the Labyrinth. She was sure there were no cars in the back of Blake Manor, and she discovered she was right.

"You can't be serious." She exclaimed, completely astonished by the contraption before her.

"Oh, I'm very serious." Dustin said, smiling, as he walked over and opened the door to his helicopter.

Dustin looked over at Nadia as she took in the sites below them. He was doing a short fly over Houston. He wanted to share this experience with her. There was nothing like the bird's-eye view of the city. He eventually landed his helicopter on the helipad of a building in downtown Houston. The building was the most capable and reasonable location to land when he conducted business in Houston. The building itself was closed, but he had access to the roof, and the view was spectacular. The air held a nice breeze as he assisted Nadia out of his helicopter. He led her over to a stairwell. The small railing allowed for support, as they could look over the city. Dustin stood two stairs below her, leaning on the railing. At his height, he was almost at eye level with her. Neither of them spoke for a while. He smiled inwardly, watching as she took in the sight of the buildings below. He couldn't help but notice she still looked very much like the teenage girl he'd fallen in love with. Her cocoa brown skin, almond-shaped brown eyes, full cheeks, and plumped lips. Her hair seemed shorter, or maybe it was the way the soft curls fanned her face. Eventually, she took a seat on the top step and looked at him.

"Do you come here often?" She asked. He slightly chuckled at her attempt to make small talk. It was a start.

"Yes, mainly for business."

"What kind of business do you do?"

"I'm involved in a few different ventures, but I guess you could say I'm into gadgets." She nodded, and he watched as she appeared unsure of how much she should ask him. This wouldn't be easy, but he wanted her comfortable enough to ask him anything. No matter what it was. Tricia had been a very direct, not beating around the bush type person, so he thought he might try being straightforward with her.

"Why don't you ask me what you really want to know?" Dustin stated.

"I don't even know where to start?" She said. Sensing her nervousness, thinking maybe him standing while she sat, was a bit intimidating. He took a seat on the step in front of her, then tried another approach.

"Close your eyes." He said gently. She gave him a suspicious look, and he further encouraged her.

"Trust me." Uncertainty still in her eyes, she did as he asked.

"Take a deep breath, that's it, now another one, perfect. Now open your eyes." She did, and her brown ones connected with his gray ones.

"Ask me." He stated flatly.

"Why didn't you come to find me? Why did you believe I was dead?" The question shocked him as much as it seemed to shock her.

"I'm sorry. I shouldn't have…." She tried to explain, but he interrupted her.

"It's fine. I told you, you could ask me anything, and I meant that." She nodded as his eyes never left hers. He took a deep breath and spoke.

"I was in Mexico when the accident happened. When I returned two weeks later, I found out you were gone." It was the hardest thing he'd come to accept.

"But we were already married?" She asked. He nodded, not sure where her mind was going.

"How could we not talk for two weeks?"

"I was visiting my grandfather. It was the year after I lost my mother. He lives in a small house outside Cancun city limits. There isn't much reception out there."

"How did you find out I was…gone?" She asked.

"The minute I got off the plane and turned my phone back on. I had several messages from Tanya." He answered. Events from that day flowed through his mind as if they had just happened.

"Who's Tanya?" She asked, interrupting his thoughts. He would need to tell her about her best friend at some point. Now that he was thinking about it, it might be a good time to reach out to Tanya.

"Tanya is your best friend, or she was Tricia's best friend. Sorry. It takes some getting used to." He had to work on keeping Nadia and Tricia separate in his mind.

"I'm beginning to see what you mean." She said, he continued.

"After trying to read through all of Tanya's messages filled with panic and worry, I finally called her, and she told me you died in an accident. She also told me your parents had a funeral...that I missed." He said. The pain of not saying goodbye hurt more than he could ever convey.

"Oh my gosh. Why would they do that if you were my husband?" She asked. He rubbed his hand around the back of his neck before he answered.

"They didn't know." Her eyes widened at the bomb he'd just dropped on her. He wasn't surprised. They'd married in secret. It was only supposed to be that way until she graduated. Nothing had gone to plan.

"Why wouldn't they know?"

"We didn't tell them." He answered. She looked at him with her mouth agape, and he tensed, figuring he knew the thoughts she was thinking.

"Was I pregnant?" She asked. Okay, he was wrong. That was the last thing he thought she was thinking.

"No, you weren't pregnant." He answered. He didn't want to explain that they hadn't had sex until their actual wedding night. They grew quiet after that, and she asked him to take her back to the Manor. He obliged. They didn't need to talk about everything that day. He also knew, trying to pile a lifetime of memories into one afternoon would put anyone on the brink of insanity. Dustin was still wrapping his mind around the fact that she was alive. Once they arrived back at Blake Manor, she talked with Ashiree before saying her goodbyes. She didn't object to him walking her to her car. She also gave him her phone number and promised to text him when she made it home safely. Despite the tension and uneasiness in their conversation, he enjoyed being around her. A part of him wanted to run after her car as she pulled out of the gate from Blake Manor, but he didn't want to crowd her. He did, however, want to spend more time with her. Walking back into Blake Manor, once he could no longer see the taillights of her car, he thought of inviting her to his ranch. He wanted her to see it. Smiling, he decided to ask her. The worse she could say was no. But he had a funny feeling, she just might say yes.

Dustin at Seventeen:

Dustin noticed the moment Tricia snuck into the barn. The weather seemed to whimper and howl alongside Gretel as she echoed her pain, bringing her colt into the world. Brett and a few other ranchers were around for the birth also. Hansel neighed in his stall next to his sister, also expressing his sympathies.

"Did I miss anything?" She asked, stripping out of her soaked sweater. It was very humid in the barn despite the rain outside cooling the temperature.

"No, nothing exciting yet." Dustin said, standing to kiss her temple then turning back to Gretel.

"Hey, girl. How's she doing, Brett?" Tricia asked.

"She seems to be doing well so far, but it could be a long night. Waiting on colts and fillies is a process." Dustin watched Tricia's face beam with pride as Brett spoke about Gretel's new addition coming into the world. He watched as Gretel staggered between lying down and standing back up. Brett explained that her behavior was normal, but every time she would lie down, Dustin's heart beat a little faster, anticipating the moment. They were all giving Gretel some distance to help the process take its natural course. The continued howling of the wind and the downpour of the rain pounding on the barn increased the surrounding anxiety.

"I think it's time." He heard Brett say. Dustin and Tricia both noticed a tiny hoof sticking out in a cream-like sack. But after a few more seconds, Gretel stood again.

"That looks awfully uncomfortable." Tricia said. A few of the ranchers chuckled.

"It's actually quite normal." Brett stated.

"How long will she walk around like that?" Tricia asked.

"Normally, that's a good sign that soon she will finish giving birth, but I've known some mares to go for hours." Dustin felt Tricia shudder at the site. He leaned down to whisper in her ear.

"Making you rethink all those kids you want." He teased.

"Shut up, Dusty." She answered playfully, swatting at his chest. The other ranchers laughed at their teasing of each other until Gretel finally laid down, and with slight huffs, she birthed her foal into the world.

"Oh my goodness. Look at him, Dusty."

"I see, Trixie." He smiled at her excitement as they watched the new foal begin to wobble a little, attempting to stand. He saw a concerned look on Brett's face as he softly spoke to another rancher.

"What's wrong?" Dustin asked.

"Not sure yet." Brett answered.

"Come on, ole girl." He heard one of the ranchers say. Gretel should have stood back up by now, helping and encouraging her young one.

"Men." Tricia rolled her eyes and huffed. "You expect her to just recover immediately after pushing her baby out." Brett smiled at Tricia's comment, but Dustin knew that was normal. Slight fear began to rise in him over the next few minutes as one rancher continued whispering to Gretel, encouraging her to stand. She finally did, a sigh of relief expelled from Dustin. Her foal slowly mimicked her movements and stood on his own. They all clapped and continued to watch the bond form between mother and baby.

"His coat is like a dull charcoal, and it reminds me of a hockey puck." Tricia said nonchalantly. A few of the ranchers looked over at them and smiled.

"His coat will fill in later." Brett replied.

"But I like the name." Another rancher said.

"What name?" Dustin asked.

"Hockey Puck." He answered, winking at Tricia. She beamed back at him. A few others nodded, and as if in total agreement, the young foal neighed softly.

"Well, since he appears to agree with you, Hockey Puck it is."

Chapter Eight

Nadia took a deep breath as the car came to a stop in front of a Two-Story mid-size house on the westside of Houston. This was her childhood home. Looking through her passenger side window, she squinted her eyes to see if anything seemed familiar or sparked a memory. She got nothing.

"Are you sure you're up for this?" She looked over at Donnell and nodded slowly. She'd asked him to come with her. She was sure Dustin wouldn't have minded coming but knowing her parents hadn't been too fond of him, she decided against it. Donnell was kind enough to help her find her parents and set up a time to meet them. She wasn't too sure why she'd felt so calm around him, but he put her at ease. Taking another deep breath, she opened her car door the same time Donnell did and exited the car. Upon closing it, she saw the front door to the house open, and a man and a woman came to step out onto the porch. Nadia looked over to Donnell, who'd circled the car and was now standing next to her. Nodding his head in encouragement, she strolled up to the house.

"Oh my gosh, I can't believe it." She heard the woman say and instantly stepped off the last two steps engulfing her in a hug. Nadia was a little taken back but unsure of why. Wouldn't it be natural for any mom to want to hug their child, especially if they assumed the child was dead? The woman pulled back, and Nadia tried her best to smile as the woman cupped her face with her hands.

"I can't believe my Tricia is alive." Nadia slightly flinched at being called Tricia.

"Aileen, why don't you give the girl some space." She heard the gentlemen, she assumed was her dad, say. His robust voice startled Nadia for just a second, but she was thankful when Aileen, her mother, took a couple of steps back. What was wrong with her? These were her parents. She should feel thrilled and excited to see them finally. To know that she wasn't abandoned. Shouldn't her heart be leaping with joy that she was no longer alone? She smiled as best she could as her father, John, introduced himself with a handshake, clearly noticing how uncomfortable she was with the hug from her mother. He also shook Donnell's hands as Aileen ushered them to come into the house. Taking the two steps to stand on the porch, she felt Donnell's hands on her upper back. She looked over at him.

"Are you sure you're alright?" He asked.

"I don't know." She answered him honestly. She didn't know how to explain what she was feeling at this moment. The way this reunion played in her head several times before they arrived was nothing like what she felt now. She thought she'd be ecstatic, alleviated to reunite with her parents finally, but she wasn't. What was wrong with her?

"Nothing." She heard Donnell say, only then realizing she'd spoken out loud.

"Every situation is different. You haven't seen your parents for twelve years, and you don't remember anything about them. I'm sure it's natural to feel a little disconnected. Don't put too much pressure on yourself. This is a lot to take in."

"Thanks, Donnell." She said while exhaling slowly to calm her nerves. Taking one more step, she opened the screen door, and with Donnell behind her, she entered her childhood home.

Dustin exited his room at Blake Manor when he saw Shannon and Kelsey. Kelsey was holding a vase almost as big as she was.

"Would you like some help with that?" He offered.

"Hello, Dustin. Thank you, but no." Kelsey greeted him with a pleasant smile.

"I hope she doesn't drop it." Shannon stated with a warning.

"That looks rather heavy." Dustin said.

"Oh, it's not as heavy as it looks, but it could be very important." Kelsey beamed.

"Ashiree hired Kelsey to redecorate the Manor, and she's becoming obsessed with some of my grandmother's vases."

"She collected vases! How cool is that?" Dustin chuckled a little at Kelsey's enthusiasm and Shannon's slight annoyance.

"Dominic mentioned that. Congratulations."

"Thank you. So, how are things going with you and Nadia?" Kelsey asked.

"I've invited her to spend a couple of weeks at my ranch with me."

"Awe, that's so sweet. I hope you two work things out." Kelsey said, readjusting her grip on the vase.

"That's it." Shannon interrupted. "Marvin!" She called out to one of the staff members. He arrived quickly, almost appearing out of the blue.

"Yes, Ms. Walden?"

"Please take this vase to the living area beside the wine cellar for Ms. Jewel."

"Shannon! I said I have it." Kelsey declared.

"Give him the vase. We have plenty of hands around here for you not to do any heavy lifting." Kelsey reluctantly handed over the vase.

"Thank you, Marvin. I have two others I need to move as well." Kelsey said grudgingly.

"Yes, ma'am. If you show me which ones, I'll be happy to move them for you." Marvin retreated down the stairs with the vase in his hand.

"See how easy that was." Shannon explained.

"I could have handled it." Kelsey protested.

"Kelsey, if you want to own your own company one day, you have to learn how to delegate." Shannon's phone rang, interrupting her talk to Kelsey. "I have to take this. Dustin, it was great seeing you again." She said, answering her phone and heading down the stairway. Kelsey turned toward Dustin after Shannon left.

"She's always so bossy." Kelsey jokingly complained.

"True, but she has a point. Delegation is very important."

"I guess you're right." Kelsey pouted. Dustin chuckled as Marvin returned up the stairs. "Well, back to work for me. I wish all the best of luck for you and Nadia." Dustin thanked her as she directed Marvin to the other vases. He eventually found his way downstairs and saw Dominic sitting at the desk in his office.

"You look deep in thought." Dustin said, announcing his presence.

"I do not know how anyone could work at home every day." Dominic complained.

"Technically, I worked at home." Dustin responded. Taking a seat in front of the glass top desk.

"How much time do you actually spend inside your home besides sleeping?"

"Point taken." Dustin said, knowing Dominic was right. "You should come out to the ranch sometime?" Dustin stated. He hadn't noticed until that very moment that he never actually invited Dominic to his ranch. Darwin visited a few times, mainly unannounced. Dillon, Donnell and Dexter visited right after the Equestrian opened, and even Damien visited. Of course, it was for one of his many photoshoots and had it been any other person, Dustin would have said no.

"I might take you up on that offer." Dominic said.

"Anytime, just let me know." Dustin responded, and then he watched Dominic put down the report he was reading and rest back in his chair.

"Have you heard from Donnell yet?"

"Not yet. I'm sure Nadia's still visiting her parents."

"How do you think that's going?"

"For her sake, I hope it's going well." Dustin answered honestly. He'd offered out of pure kindness to go with Nadia to see her parents. She respectively declined but agreed to have Donnell with her. Dustin was fine with that decision.

"You don't sound too confident." Dominic said.

"Let's just say they weren't the biggest cheerleaders for our relationship." Dustin answered. He hadn't seen her parents since after Tricia's funeral, and the dismissive tones from her mother hit harder than he wanted to admit. It actually hurt, thinking of all the events that occurred the year before.

Dustin at Seventeen:

Dustin watched with a heavy heart as Hockey Puck was being led onto the trailer. Gretel didn't get better after birthing Puck. Brett escorted two veterinarians in to see her. Listening to her wheezing and straining to breathe broke his heart. There was nothing he could do, nothing he knew to do to help. Fifteen hours later, she was gone. Dustin stayed with her until the end. Watching her inhale and exhale her last breath. Sorrow like nothing he'd ever felt surrounded him. Even Hansel neighed, in painful agony, mourning the life of his twin. Hockey Puck whined as well, missing his mother.

"Wait! Wait!" He turned to see Tricia running toward them. She went straight to the trailer and held two bars with her hands.

"You can't let them take him." she said to Brett.

"It's out of our hands, Tricia. Without Gretel, Puck can't survive. We don't have any mares here to produce milk."

"Where are they taking him?"

"To another farm with a couple of nursing mares." He watched her look back into the trailer. The driver indicated he needed to leave, and Brett looked at Dustin to help with Tricia. He took the three steps to her.

"Come on, Trixie, we have to let him go." He watched her shake her head and then gripped the bars tighter.

"Please, Tricia, he won't survive here." He watched her slowly loosen her grip. She placed her hand, threw the bars, palm flat and waited a few seconds before Hockey Puck came and lifted his head to her palm, and she scratched lightly.

"Goodbye, Puck." She finally said, taking a step back and watching as the trailer began to roll away. Dustin put his arms around Tricia's shoulder as they watched the trailer disappear until the faint sight of the dust remained. Thirty minutes later, Dustin lay with Tricia in his arms. They were in a storage area above Gretel's stall that Tricia had deemed their secret spot. The side of the space looked directly over into the stall. Once they couldn't see the trailer on the road pulling away, they walked into the barn, climbed the side stairs completely covered with hay, and cried. Losing Gretel hurt more than he could say. She was the reason camp became such a joy to him. He looked forward to spending every moment in the barn with her. This whole summer was hard; first, his mom died, then Gretel and now Puck was gone. It was a lot to take on. With Tricia in his arms, her shutters and cries seem to fade slowly. He could hear Hansel huffing in his stall. Did animals feel what humans felt? What must it have been like for Hansel to lose his sister and now his nephew? Did animals have relationships like they did? Tricia shifted, breaking his thought pattern.

"I'm going to find him one day." Dustin held her tighter but said nothing. He knew she needed to vent.

"I'm going to find him and take care of him and tell him what a wonderful mother he'd had." He felt a teardrop from her face through the opening of his shirt and onto his chest.

"Will you help me?" She asked, looking up at him, with fresh tears forming in her eyes. He never saw her cry before today. Tricia's tough exterior kept her guarded and in control, but his girl had a soft side, a tender side. He hated seeing the tears, hearing the sorrow in her voice, feeling the tension of uncertainty in her body.

"You know I will."

"You have to promise, Dusty." She sat up a little, her eyes connecting with his with sheer determination in them. "When we get our farm, we'll find him." she added. A part of him knew that by the time they were old enough to have the life he so badly wanted to give her, finding Puck would be practically an impossible task. But he couldn't deny her anything, and he'd give her the world if he could. They had their whole lives in front of them, and if she wanted to search to the end of the earth to find Puck when they got older, then he'd be right beside her. He wiped a tear away with his thumb and placed a strand of her hair that was blowing slightly from the breeze in the barn back behind her ear.

"I promise."

Chapter Nine

"**Two weeks**! You're spending two weeks with him." Kyle traced Nadia's every step from her closet to her bed, packing her suitcase.

"Yes, Kyle, he invited me to his ranch for two weeks."

"And you agreed to this." she nodded. She had. She hated being placed in this position. Kyle had a right to be upset. His world was affected by this chain of events, but what was she supposed to do? She had a whole life she knew nothing about.

"How am I, as your fiancé, supposed to feel about this?"

"Probably the same way my husband does." She paused instantly at her words.

She never spoke up, never talked back. Where had that come from? She looked over at Kyle, who seemed just as taken back by her comment as she had. Dropping the shirt in her hand into the suitcase, she went back into her closet and grabbed a few more items.

"So, he's your husband now?" She heard Kyle spat. She took a deep breath, excited her closet, and went over to her dresser.

"I don't want to argue with you."

"Fine." She watched him storm out of her room and heard the front door slam. She wished she could make him understand. This wasn't about Dustin or even him. It was about her. She needed answers. Some that only Dustin seemed to provide. The visit with her parents was weird. They practically refused to discuss anything about the last time they saw her. She wasn't an expert at reading people, but something didn't seem right. It was hard to explain. They mentioned her accomplishments, and she had plenty, or rather Tricia had plenty. Tricia Hanson was a genius compared to who she was now. She was a 4.0 student, granted several awards and achievements, but what about her hobbies? Her dreams? Her desires? They were very proud parents. They praised and raved about this grand plan they had for their daughter, but what did Tricia actually want? She asked them, and they both seemed surprised by the question as if their daughter's wants wouldn't differ from theirs. It made her wonder for a second if maybe she wasn't the happy little girl her parents were portraying her to be. She also asked about Tanya, and her parents seem not to have the best opinion of Tanya, claiming Tanya would also get her into trouble and was a bad influence on her. So, her parents didn't approve of Tanya, didn't seem to know a single intimate detail about her, and did not know why she'd married Dustin.

Placing her last items in her suitcase, she zipped it up and rolled it to her living room. She found it ironic that she could pack up her suitcase for two weeks, leave her apartment and have nothing to worry about. There was no one to call, no animals or plants to be concerned with. She didn't even have mail delivered. Every bill she had was electronically sent. She didn't talk to her neighbors, and most were consumed with their own lives, kids, spouse, crazy exes and family drama. She did one last walk through her bedroom, ensuring that everything was in place, not that anyone would know. She grabbed her suitcase and headed to her car. Dustin offered to get her transportation to Blake Manor, but she wanted to drive. Something about driving soothed her. Although she could admit, Houston traffic had its own annoyances. Other drivers constantly cut her off or refused to use their blinker, expecting her to read their minds when they wanted to switch lanes. After placing her suitcase on her back seat, she turned on the engine and was about to connect her Bluetooth to her car, intending on playing her playlist, when a song began playing on the oldies but goodies station. She couldn't recall where she'd heard it before, but it seemed so familiar. She asked Siri for the details on the song and downloaded it. Deciding to leave the radio on the same station, she headed for Blake Manor.

Kyle watched Nadia pull out of the parking lot and shook his head. Why his mother insisted on him marrying her, he didn't know. This wasn't even supposed to be his life, and this wasn't his dream. He drove his car out of the parking lot, heading in the opposite direction. She wanted to go be with the cowboy then fine by him. He didn't chase women, never had, never would. He knew his mother wanted him to play the doting over caring fiancé, but he was done. He never wanted this anyway, any of it. He was stressed and completely annoyed by the turn of events in the last month. He honestly wasn't upset about not marrying Nadia. She was boring, beautiful, but boring. There was no fire in her at all. He believed that was one thing his mother loved about her. She didn't push back, and she was easy-going, in some ways, a complete doormat. It didn't matter. She wasn't what he wanted, and she would never be what he wanted. If Nadia was going to discover whatever her life had been with the so-called husband, that was fine by him. He told Siri to call a number.

"Hello."

"Hey, you."

"What do you want, Kyle?" He smiled, knowing she knew exactly what he wanted.

"You, as always."

"Um-hm, sure you do. This wouldn't have anything to do with your fiancé
finding out she has a husband, would it?"

"It has everything to do with that. She chose him over me. I think you should help mend my broken heart." He heard her laugh, and he couldn't help but chuckle at the act himself.

"I don't believe you are heartbroken at all."

"I'm not, but I'm good at pretending." he listened to her laugh again and loved it. Why couldn't his mom have chosen her? She was perfect for him.

"I'll meet you at our spot in twenty minutes."

"Okay...Oh, and Margery?"

"Yes, Kyle."

"Don't wear any panties."

Dustin watched Nadia's face as he did a fly-over of his property. She saw a bird's-eye view of the open land, the house, the stables, and the Equestrian. The excitement on her face warmed his heart. Everything in and on his property resembled a life he wanted to create for the woman he loved. A life that was cut short before they really had a chance to live it. But they had dreams, goals, desires, and other things they wanted to share with one another. Despite her having none of her memories, he still wanted to share it with her. He wanted to show her all that he had accomplished. Landing the helicopter on the north end of the property not too far from the house, he assisted Nadia in stepping out and then walked over to his home.

"This is incredible. You have so much open space out here." She exclaimed. He smiled. It was one thing he loved most. The openness, the seclusion, completely different from the thriving environment of city life in Houston.

"Thank you. I hope you enjoy it while you're here."

"I plan to, but I have a confession to make."

"Really? What's that?"

"I've never been on a horse." She said, then paused with deepened brows. "Or have I?" Dustin tried to hide his laugh as they entered the back porch of his house.

"Yes, you've been on a horse, at least as Tricia you have. But don't worry. I'll have you mounted on a horse once or twice before your stay ends." He said, opening the back door and escorting her in.

"Welcome to my humble abode." He heard her slightly chuckle. The farmhouse was massive, simple in design, but spacious. He explained the layout. The two-story house consisted of five bedrooms, three of which had their own connecting bath. A double-sized master, a larger living area, a kitchen with a nook, a formal dining room and a family den with a built-in fireplace.

Neither could ignore the aroma coming from the kitchen as they entered the house.

"Are you cooking something?"

"I'm sure Ms. Anita is whipping something up. Come on, let me introduce you." He walked down a hall and into the kitchen. Sure enough, he found Ms. Anita with her hands completely covered in flour, kneading what he could only assume was dough for biscuits.

"Good evening Ms. Anita."

"Dustin." She exclaimed, abandoning her task and wiping her hands on a towel.

"I thought I heard the chopper overhead. And just who do we have here?"

"Ms. Anita, this is Nadia. Nadia, this is my saving grace, Ms. Anita."

"Oh, stop that." She said, waving him off. "We both know you are more my saving grace than I was yours." Dustin smiled as she walked over to hug Nadia.

"Sorry, dear, I'm kind of a hugger. It's nice to meet you."

"Thank you, and it's nice to meet you too. Whatever you're making smells amazing."

"Dustin! Did you not feed her?"

"And have her miss out on the best cook this side of heaven?"

"Sweet Talker." Ms. Anita said, eyeing him skeptically. "Go round up those boys of yours. Dinner is almost ready." Dustin shook his head and laughed.

"And here I thought I was the boss." he said to Nadia, who smiled back at him.

"Oh please, we all know the true bosses around here are those horses you love so much." Ms. Anita turned to check the food and removed some biscuits from the oven.

"I'll show Nadia where she's sleeping, and then I'll round up the troops."

"Well, don't be too long. You know those boys hate cold biscuits." Dustin chuckled and led Nadia upstairs.

Dustin age Eighteen:
"You can't be serious?"

"What? It's not a bad idea. It's not like we're not going to get married, eventually."

"Eventually is not today?"

"What is really stopping us?" Dustin rubbed his hand down his face and sat on the bed in the hotel room he was sharing with Ethan. He knew there had been a reason Tricia insisted on him attending her senior spring break trip. Married. She wanted them to get married. Not that he didn't want to marry her. He knew their relationship would lead there eventually, but now? He wasn't sure. Tricia had her goals and plans of what she wanted and was confident about how she wanted her life to go. In all honesty, he didn't have everything planned out.

"Level with me Tricia, why now?"

"Because we're here, and the opportunity is presenting itself." He quirked a questioning eyebrow at her. Yesterday, they were cruising the streets of Austin with Tanya and Ethan, tucked in the corner between a few shops was a small chapel. Curiosity getting the best of Tricia, she practically drugged him by the hand, and they entered the small chapel. A nice lady smiled, greeted them, and Tricia asked all about their private ceremonies with Tanya's encouragement. He and Ethan both stood off to the sides, arms folded in complete dismay. Since leaving the chapel, it was all Tricia and Tanya talked about, which led Dustin to believe this had not been a coincidence, that she wanted him to come on this trip with her.

"Not good enough, Trixie." She stopped pacing and stared at him.

"So, you don't want us to get married." She stated flatly.

"Don't do that. If you cannot be upfront with me about why this is so important to you now, then we can drop it." He folded his arms while looking over at her. Something was going on, and he needed her to be completely forthcoming with him.

"My parents gave me an ultimatum. They found out I was planning to do a double major."

"What's the ultimatum?" He watched her look down at the floor, shuffling her heel back and forth, before taking a deep breath and looking back up at him. This would not be good.

"That I give up my dream of becoming a veterinarian or they refuse to pay for college." She said.

"Would they really do that?"

"Yes, Dustin, they would." he watched her sit defeatedly on the bed beside him, shoulders slouched. She looked tired at that moment. This ongoing battle with her parents wasn't something new. The more she tried to please them, the more they demanded from her.

"How does us getting married fix that, Trixie?" he had to be upfront. He wanted Tricia in his life, always. That he knew for sure, but marriage was a lot to take on when he wasn't even sure what he wanted out of life.

"The life insurance policy my grandmother left me." She said plainly, looking over at him.

"I thought you said you couldn't touch that until you were twenty-five."

"I can't unless I'm married."

"Your grandmother put that in as a stipulation?"

"I don't think so intentionally. It's just in the legal jargon."

"How'd you find that out?"

"Let's just say it pays to have a friend who wants to be a lawyer and knows how to read the small print." He smiled, knowing she was talking about Tanya.

"I would think if your parents knew they wouldn't let you read the will." He watched her shuffle her heel and then smiled at him.

"I sort of broke into my dad's safe." Dustin shook his head and laughed out loud. Of course, she did.

"I can't live like this anymore, Dusty. I know I'm asking a lot. But please. You know I hate begging."

"So, you're not worried about me marrying you for your money?" He said teasingly. She playfully swatted at him.

"Not with who your father is." She countered. He leaned over to kiss her sweetly on the lips.

"Are you sure this is what you want?" She nodded. Dustin let out a slow breath as he made his decision. His Trixie needed help, his help, and he knew there wasn't anything he wouldn't do for. Looking into her pleading eyes, he spoke.

"Then it looks like you, Tricia Hanson, are getting a husband." She threw her hands around his neck and kissed him hard. He smiled against her lips, wrapping his arms around her.

"I love you, Dusty Gray." She proclaimed happily after ending their kiss. He smiled at her and leaned back on the bed, taking her with him. She giggled a little, a sound he rarely heard from her unless she was happy.

"I love you too, Trixie."

Chapter Ten

Nadia sighed as she walked onto the back porch of the house. The last two days with Dustin were more than she ever could have expected. She knew he lived on the outskirts of San Antonio and owned a lot of land, but she hadn't been prepared for the site. Green pastures were everywhere. It went on for miles. She'd never seen so much open land. At least she did not remember if she had. Taking a stand next to one of the posts and resting her elbow on the railing, she sighed again. That was the hardest part about being here. There were so many memories and history between Dustin and a woman she no longer knew. She honestly grew uncomfortable with him sharing memories of what used to be the two of them. He seemed so taken with who she was, and if she were honest, she'd gotten a little jealous, which was absolutely ridiculous. Nadia wasn't sure how to handle the feelings stirring inside of her. It was truly like her heart knew more than her head, which was partially true. She felt a comfort with Dustin she'd never felt with anyone else, and that actually scared her.

This afternoon was one of those moments. Today they'd visited the Horse Equestrian. She'd never heard of horse healing before. Her idea of what it could look like was completely blown away by the resort-style building and barn she'd approached earlier. A full staff of servers, hosts, cooks, and patrons occupied a nice part of the west-end of his property. She thought she'd see a stable with a couple of horses, but it had been so much more. Dustin oversaw an entirely unprecedented experience with horses. She was pleasantly surprised by the number of actual residents living at the Equestrian, many with various conditions like depression, anxiety, eating disorders and even post-traumatic stress. The manager, Julia, further explained how the entire operation worked, the success stories tied to the Equestrian and the history of the five years it took fighting with the state to get the entire thing up and running. After listening to Julia and receiving her own private tour of the compound, Nadia had a newfound respect for Dustin. The Equestrian was phenomenal and something she'd never even known there was a need for. That admiration quickly shifted to an increasing attraction she was tired of fighting. Her desire to see him, learn more about him, only grew. The true crux of her problem is she wanted him, all of him. But she knew his heart belonged to a woman that didn't exist anymore. She couldn't be her, didn't even know where to start if she could. It scared her to think that Dustin wouldn't ever be able to accept her as Nadia.

"Hey! I wondered where you'd run off to." Dustin said, stepping onto the porch and slightly startling her.

"I just wanted to get some fresh air before dinner was ready."

"Are you alright? Did you enjoy the Equestrian?"

"Oh my gosh, yes. It's amazing. Julia gave me a full tour. It was wonderful."

"I'm glad you enjoyed it." He said, coming to stand beside the other post and leaning on the railing. Silence hung between them as the sun slowly began to descend.

"Julia told me you had some issues, in the beginning, trying to get it up and running."

"Yes, we did." He said, lightly chuckling as he explained the situation further. She never thought she'd meet a man with a smile perfect enough to star in a toothpaste commercial. Between his eyes and his smile, she was a goner.

"I think it's great how much you love horses."

"They were, and are, easier to get along with than people." Dustin answered.

"I find that hard to believe with all the friends you have."

"I guess you have a point there."

"Ashiree told me you all met in college." She knew based on the timeframe this was after he'd met Tricia and after the accident.

Information about him that didn't involve who she used to be made it easier to talk with him.

"We did. We all pledged for the same fraternity."

"Really? That sounds interesting."

"You could say that."

"Did you guys make the cut?"

"Actually, no, we didn't." He said with a mild smirk.

"Wow, none of you?"

"We were all in the same pledge group."

"Oh! Kind of a 'we win together, or we lose together' type of thing."

"Exactly."

"So, did you have any crazy embarrassing pranks to do?"

"Not nearly as much as the other guys." Nadia listened as Dustin described the task and pranks put on by two other sets of pledges. Themes like The Seventh Son of the Seventh Son and the Seven Deadly Sins. She threw her head back and laughed when Dustin explained the guys had to wear pregnant bellies for three days around campus to represent the sin 'gluttony'.

"So, what did you guys have to do that was embarrassing?"

"Well, here's the thing, our names were supposed to be our embarrassment."

"I don't get it."

"Our theme was the Seven dwarfs." Dustin stated. Nadia threw her head back and laughed again.

"Oh, that's just classic." She said, still laughing.

"Yeah, but it didn't go as the fraternity would have hoped."

"What do you mean?"

"My roommate, who was Donnie, told them he was way too tall ever to be considered a dwarf. Which is true for his 6'7' height." Nadia nodded in understanding as Dustin continued.

"So, they let us change it to the Seven Giants. We still each had a nickname from the seven dwarfs, but it wasn't as embarrassing for us as they hoped."

"Why? What happened?"

"Lots of things. For one, Dillon threw a party, almost like Halloween, demanding everyone attending to dress in some type of fairytale creature. It was actually a hit, but the frat boys didn't like the fact that we were actually embracing our new nicknames."

"So, what happened then?"

"They disqualified us, saying we broke the rules."

"What? Did you guys actually break the rules?"

"In a way, yes. The point was for us to call ourselves by our dwarfs' names if anyone approached us or spoke to us. But with Dillon throwing a party announcing to everyone what our names were, any and everyone was easily calling us by our dwarf names, not to mention the rumor Damien started."

"Which was?"

"That we were giants...in every sense of the word."

"Oh." Nadia said shyly, trying to hide a blush she knew was forming on her face.

"So..." she started saying, making sure to get her bearings together. "...what was your dwarf name?"

"Doc."

"Oh, you got the least embarrassing name."

"Maybe, but it came with its own set of problems."

"How so?"

"Let's just say there were a few women on campus wanting to play doctor."

"And did you play doctor with some of those women?" She asked curiously, trying to ignore the slight jealousy that seemed to creep up inside her. The thought of Dustin being with another woman didn't sit well with her. She didn't even like thinking of him being with her former self. She shook her head at how ridiculous she sounded.

"No, but it was a nice distraction for a while." Dustin said.

"Why did you need a distraction?" She watched his face alter to something somewhat sorrow or anguish. He turned to look out in the dark as the sun finally set. She noticed the lights for the porch cascaded a shadow of him in the grass before he turned his head to look back over at her.

"From losing everyone I loved."

Aileen Hanson walked into an office, shut the door and took a seat in front of a massive oak desk. The decor in the office seemed more fitting for a man than for the woman sitting behind it.

"I do not understand the reason for having me summoned." She began while placing her purse on the floor beside her.

"I heard you had a visitor the other day."

"What? Are you having me watched now?" Aileen griped.

"It appears you need to be watched. I thought we agreed, no contact with Nadia."

"First of all, that was your rule. Second of all, that's hard to do when she has someone else reach out to you. I couldn't just ignore it."

"Does this someone have a name?"

"Donnell, I think. He never said his last name."

"Well, isn't that helpful?" The woman across the desk snared.

"Don't go blaming me. Wasn't it your job to ensure no one knew she was alive?" Aileen countered. The woman behind the desk glared at her before speaking again.

"Yes. That was my job, which I was doing quite well. But it seems you were not forthcoming in all the information that I needed to ensure that.

"What could I have possibly left out?" She asked.

"Think really hard."

"Seriously, Lyanne. I do not know what you're talking about." She handed her an envelope. Opening it up slowly, Aileen looked at a document titled 'Certificate of Marriage'. Her hand instantly went to her mouth.

"We gave Tricia explicit instructions to stay away from him." Aileen defended.

"Well, clearly, you failed." Lyanne countered. "However, the real question is why you didn't mention she got married."

"We didn't find out until after the funeral. By that time, we all agreed to sever ties."

"And you didn't think to tell me when Kyle began dating her?"

"I figured you had it all under control." Aileen said, settling back in her chair. Lyanne exhaled a sharp breath.

"Did she appear to remember anything?" Lyanne asked.

"No, she asked a lot of vague questions. Honestly, I was just happy to see her." Aileen answered with a subtle smile.

"Clearly, your happiness distracted you from understanding the detriment of you having contact with her. Not to mention this husband of hers." Lyanne stated.

"You're so overdramatic, Lyanne. Seriously. What's so important about this Dustin Shaw?" She asked, allowing her slight frustration to etch in her voice.

"Have you been living under a rock the last twelve years?"

"You know I have been doing some soul searching, Lyanne. I have even gotten into holistic healing." Aileen stated proudly.

"Hoping to rid yourself of the demons about to erupt all around us?" Aileen sneered at Lyanne's question.

"Dustin Shaw is the late Preston Shaw's son. He lives his life pretty low-key, but I saw his pure determination at the wedding. Whatever you did with Tricia to keep her away from him didn't work, and I doubt, now that he knows she's alive, he won't be letting her out of his sight anytime soon. And that's not even the major issue."

"What do you mean?"

"One of his good friends is Dominic Blake." Dominic Blake was a name Aileen recognized. There was no way you could live anywhere near Houston or Texas and not know the Blake family name.

"I'm sure you're going to tell me how that connection affects us."

"Dominic Blake was named CEO of Gateway Pharmaceuticals a year ago." Her eyes blanched. That wasn't good. Not good at all.

"And it seems Nadia has befriended Ashiree Blake. Even if we could somehow get her away from Dustin, with Ashiree Blakes' kidnapping and two of Gateways' employees being killed last year, Dominic Blake will not let another employee go missing without massive repercussions." Lyanne said. Aileen looked at Lyanne deep in thought before speaking again.

"Do you think her spending time with Dustin will cause her memory to come back?"

"I don't know, but for our sake, let's hope it doesn't."

Nadia tried to calm her nerves as she watched the silver SUV pull up and park in front of the house.

"Are you nervous?" She hadn't heard Dustin come to stand alongside her on the porch.

"Would you think less of me if I said yes?"

"Of course not. I think a little anxiety is normal." She nodded and watched a couple exit from the car. A broad shoulder, full-bearded man extended his hand, helping his wife out of the vehicle.

"Dustin! My man. It's good to see you." the man said, closing the door and walking up the porch stairs.

"Ethan, it's good to see you too. And Tanya, you look lovely as ever." Dustin shook Ethan's hand and leaned down to kiss Tanya on the cheek. Nadia's gaze never left looking at Tanya's, who seemed almost as nervous as she was.

"Would it be too awkward if I gave you a hug?" Tanya asked. Nadia nervously smiled but nodded. Tanya engulfed her in a hug. Nadia relented and leaned into her as well. She could feel fresh tears falling on her face and couldn't explain the emotion surfacing while in Tanya's arms. Love seemed to surround her as Tanya's embrace tightened. She may have none of her memories, but her heart must have known this woman was special to her. She heard Tanya sniffle a little and knew she was also crying. Tanya finally let go and stepped back. Wiping her tears but smiling hard.

"I'm sorry. This is supposed to be a happy day, and here I am with the waterworks."

"It's fine, and I'm no better." Nadia said slowly, wiping her own tears away.

"Do I get a hug too?" Ethan said teasingly.

"Oh, shut up, Ethan." Tanya countered at his teasing.

"Why don't we all step inside. I'm sure Anita almost has dinner ready." Dustin said.

"You actually have a personal cook? Now that is life." Ethan said.

"And what exactly is wrong with the personal cook you have?" Tanya questioned, placing her hands on her hips.

"Nothing, sweetheart, but giving you a break now and then would be nice." he said, leaning down and kissing her temple.

"Good save." Tanya said, relaxing her stance and allowing her husband to embrace her. Nadia smiled as she followed Dustin into the house. Ethan and Tanya's relationship started around the same time she and Dustin's had. They were still together, and even with the small bantering, she knew they still loved each other. She sighed a little as they went to freshen up before dinner, wondering if she and Dustin would have still been together if she'd never lost her memories.

Dustin watched Nadia laugh aloud as both Ethan and Tanya shared memories of all of them together as teenagers. He hadn't seen Nadia this relaxed and carefree since she'd come to the ranch. As he watched her laugh with Tanya and Ethan, he knew he'd made the right decision in contacting Tanya and asking if she and Ethan would spend a couple of days at the ranch.

"I'm so serious. I think you were more upset that Dustin hit him first for taking your swimsuit top." Tanya exclaimed. Dustin smiled as Nadia placed her hand on her head in embarrassment.

"I can't believe I used to fight boys."

"Oh, believe it. Ethan here gave you plenty of practice." Nadia's eyes widened in shock, and Ethan belted out a laugh.

"I wasn't always this hunk of a man you see now. I was pretty scrawny as a little kid." Ethan said.

"I'm so sorry." Nadia said, stifling a laugh.

"I loved those summers. They were the best times of my life as a child." Tanya sighed.

"Mine too." Dustin added.

"I wish I remembered." Nadia admitted. Dustin reached over and rubbed her arm in support.

"Well, I, for one, am kind of happy you don't." Ethan stated flatly.

"Ethan!" Tanya exclaimed, nudging him hard with her elbow.

"What? Do you have any idea how embarrassing it is to know a girl beat you until you were almost fourteen years old?" Nadia snickered again.

"Ignore him. He really means well but constantly puts his foot in his mouth."

"It's okay. It's not sitting well with me I used to beat up boys for fun."

"Oh! Don't worry too much about it. It all changed the moment you fell for Dustin." Tanya happily teased. Nadia looked over at Dustin, and he winked at her.

"I think it was more of Dustin falling for her." Ethan stated.

"How would you know? You were too busy falling for me." Tanya countered.

"I'm still falling for you, sweetheart." Tanya playfully swatted at Ethan.

"You say the sweetest things, but we all know Tricia fell first. Dustin was way too involved with the horses back then."

"Was he?" Nadia asked.

"Yes, and since Dustin loved them, you began to love them too. You practically spent every moment you could in the barn with him the last couple of summers at camp." Tanya explained. Dustin took a swig of his beer as Nadia looked over at him shyly. He'd shared with her a few memories of them being in the barn together taking care of the horses. It was where he fell in love with her.

"I can't wait to see the Equestrian." Tanya continued, interrupting his thoughts.

"You're going to love it." Nadia said with delight.

"I just think it's so sweet that after all this time, Dustin kept his promise to you." Dustin instantly froze, and he saw Nadia do the same. She turned to him with a questioning brow and then looked back over at Tanya.

"What promise?" Dustin watched Tanya's brows deepen, and then she looked over at him. Recognition finally showed in her eyes.

"You didn't tell her, did you?"

"No." Dustin answered, his eyes focusing on Nadia. She glanced back and forth between him and Tanya. Ethan shifted uncomfortably.

"Tell me what?" Nadia asked.

"I'm sorry. My husband isn't the only one to put his foot in his mouth."

"Dustin?" Nadia addressed him. "What didn't you tell me? What promise did you keep?" Dustin took a deep breath. This wasn't how he wanted her to find out. Honestly, he wasn't sure if he ever wanted her to find out.

"The Horse Equestrian. I promised you...Tricia that we'd have one." He watched several emotions play on her face. She looked down in her lap for a second, then back up to Ethan and Tanya. Then back to him, and the hurt he saw tore at his heart.

"I'm sorry." she said before she bolted out of her chair and ran out the back door.

"Oh my goodness, Dustin, I'm so sorry." Tanya explained. He stood slowly to go after Nadia.

"It's fine. I should have told her." Dustin admitted. Ms. Anita came in, her face etched with concern after hearing Nadia run out the back door. He reassured her Nadia would be fine, then asked Ms. Anita to show Ethan and Tanya what room they could settle in for the night. Excusing himself, he went after Nadia.

Chapter Eleven

Nadia stood hugging herself as the night air calmly blew past. The moon was high and cascading over the pasture. The sound of crickets echoed in the dark, and Nadia could hear the rustling of the soil as someone approached her.

"Nadia." She closed her eyes, hearing Dustin call out to her. She couldn't turn around to face him, not just yet. She couldn't face the truth about what she'd learned tonight. The truth of what she truly longed for in life. She hadn't been aware of what she truly desired until she heard him admit that he'd kept a promise to a woman he thought was dead. How much love did you have to have for someone to spend your life fulfilling a dream that wasn't even your own? The moment she realized that's exactly what he had done, she knew in her heart that's what she was missing...love. Sure, she thought Kyle loved her but did he really? She hated to make a comparison, but Kyle was the only relationship she'd had since waking up and remembering nothing about who she was before. There was no doubt in her mind that Dustin could have pushed for time with her sooner, but he'd been patient. Going so far as to invite Tanya to help shed some more light on her past. She'd learned from Margery about Dustin not giving up the property in San Antonio, which she was very certain was the ground she stood on now. The Horse Equestrian, she found so fascinating, was all in him keeping his promise to a woman he'd lost years ago. A woman she used to be. He loved her that much. That in itself was enough to understand the man that he truly was. It also made her realize how much she wanted to be that woman. How much she longed to be loved like that. Even in death. And that made her bolt from the table because in all truth... she was that woman. Whether or not she remembered didn't matter because he had done it all for her.

"Nadia." He called her name again, almost in a pleading tone for her to acknowledge him. She felt him move closer, not directly beside her, but closer. Concern and worry etched in her face as she turned to face him.

"I'm sorry I ran out."

"I'm sorry I didn't tell you."

"Why didn't you?" She watched as he stared out into the darkness before connecting his eyes to hers.

"I didn't know how or even if I wanted to."

"You didn't want me to know that you kept a promise or fulfilled a dream. A dream that was apparently mine in another life." He chuckled at her attempt to make a joke considering their situation. Sometimes the air seemed so thick between them.

"You can't tell someone their dreams, Nadia. It's like trying to tell them they love you." She nodded, understanding his reluctance.

"I wasn't ready to hear about it." She admitted.

"I know you weren't."

"I think I'm ready now." She watched the quick flash of shock on his face. But she meant it. She didn't want to tiptoe around whatever they shared. She wanted him to share all the memories of who she was before, who they were together, how they fell in love.

"Are you sure?" He asked. She nodded, smiling, completely nervous but also excited.

"Okay, we should probably get back. I'm sure Tanya is a little worried about you."

"Oh, my goodness. I completely forgot about them." Dustin quirked a brow.

"Not like that. I don't have short-term memory loss. I just meant...." She noticed Dustin teasingly laughing at her.

"Dustin." She playfully swatted at him, but he caught her hand. She immediately felt the electrical current flowing between them. She inhaled sharply as she stared back into his tantalizing gray eyes. He lightened the grip on her hand, brought her knuckles to his lips and gently kissed them.

"Let's go back in."

"Alright." She wasn't sure if she was walking or floating as they headed back into the house hand in hand.

"**This place** is amazing." Tanya exclaimed as Julia finished giving them a tour of the Equestrian.

"I'm so happy you think so." Julia said proudly. Nadia watched as Tanya asked a few more questions before Julia showed them an area they could sit quietly and have some lunch.

"I cannot believe Dustin accomplished all this." Tanya said.

"I know, it's so beautiful. I couldn't believe it was a resort for horse healing when I first arrived. It feels more like a five-star vacation resort."

"It does. If I were riding past, I would have thought that." They grew quiet for a minute, eating and taking in the surrounding scene. Tanya broke the silence first after she was practically finished with her food.

"So, question-and-answer time." Nadia smiled, loving Tanya's directness and her ability to ease her nerves. When they woke up, the four of them ate breakfast, and Tanya was very forward in telling Dustin she wanted some girl time to talk with Nadia. Nadia tried to hide her smile. She'd awaken with the same thoughts. She needed time to talk with Tanya as well.

"So, how did we meet?" Nadia asked, placing her elbow on the small bench table and resting her face on her hand.

"Oh, you want the Sandbox chronicles." She happily exclaimed. Nadia quirked a brow.

"Sandbox chronicles? What is that?" Tanya began to explain how they met in the sandbox at the park as little girls and how Tricia would throw sand and get it everywhere, to their mothers' complete and utter dismay. Nadia laughed as she listened, learning that she and Tanya had been friends since they'd met that day at the sandbox. She also learned they attended the same school and shared most of the same classes from Kindergarten through senior year.

"So, whenever someone would ask us how we met, we would say Sandbox Chronicles because that is how it began."

"That's pretty unique. Definitely an attention grabber."

"Yes, and I was all about attention."

"I take it I wasn't." Nadia answered, feeling more confident after last night. She accepted that she'd been Tricia Hanson, a vibrant, smart girl that seemed to have a complicated life with her parents but great memories with her friends.

"You didn't like attention, but you got it and a lot of it."

"Well, that hasn't changed. I still don't like a lot of attention." She said honestly.

"Oh, there was one exception to that rule. You liked the very special attention of a certain cowboy." Tanya said teasingly. She smiled back at her, knowing exactly the certain someone she was referring to.

"Dustin."

"Um-hmm." Tanya stood and stretched. "Let's walk for a minute, I don't know what it is, but walking and talking seems to go hand in hand with me." They discarded the remains of their uneaten lunch in a nearby wastebasket and walked along the property line of the Equestrian.

"So, was I boy crazy like most teenage girls?"

"Nope, that would be me." Tanya said, pointing a finger at herself.

"So, how did me and Dustin get together?" Nadia asked.

"Honestly, I am not sure." Nadia looked over at her questioningly as Tanya continued. "I mean, you literally just claimed him as your boyfriend, and that was it. It might have had a little to do with me flirting with him."

"You flirted with Dustin?"

"Yes, again, the boy crazy one." She said, pointing to herself again as they continued to walk. "Plus, he had the whole Ryan Guzman sexy cowboy thing going on." Nadia laughed at Tanya's playful description of Dustin. She agreed with the sexy cowboy thing, and he had it down for sure. They saw a bench seat not too far from where they were. It was painted orange. Julia explained to both of them that orange was seen to bring warmth and comfort. Many patrons at the Equestrian would seek to sit on it after one of their sessions. Noticing it was currently unoccupied, they chose to walk over and sit on it. Neither of them spoke for a while after they sat. Not too far in front of them, a young girl near a horse was with one trainer helping her mount. Nadia could see a woman close to the girl holding her hands in a ball at her chest. She seemed nervous, watching her daughter finally settle on a horse.

"Can I ask you a more difficult question?" Nadia began.

"Ask away." Tanya prompted.

"How were my parents?"

"Oh, we just went from Sandbox chronicles to needing bottles of wine."

"That bad, huh?" Nadia wasn't surprised by Tanya's disposition regarding her parents. They didn't seem too fond of Tanya either, yet Tanya had been her best friend.

"Not bad, just overwhelming. Your parents were really strict with you. Almost demanding you be perfect, which I never understood. Nobody is perfect, and you were very close considering everything they had you doing." Nadia listened as Tanya explained all the trophies, awards, plaques, and certificates she'd been awarded, and her parents still seemed to demand more.

They spent the next couple of hours discussing things in Tanya's life with her two boys, who were with her mom this weekend, to allow her some time to see Nadia. They were six and three and true boys at heart. Nadia also learned that Ethan had been in the army for a few years and lived on a farm like Dustin's. Not nearly as massive as Dustin's entire property covered one hundred and twenty-five acres, but still a place where her boys could roam free, get covered in dirt and scare Tanya with the creepy crawlers they seem to find outside. They continued laughing and talking until they saw Dustin and Ethan walking toward them.

"That is still the finest man I've ever laid eyes on." Tanya admitted, unashamedly ogling her husband. Nadia chuckled. Her view of Dustin wasn't too bad either.

"Don't look at me like that woman." Ethan said as they approached. "I felt like I might have to send out a search party for you."

"You're exaggerating, Ethan, and it's only been a couple of hours." Tanya responded while standing up.

"Try more like five hours." Ethan stated.

"Really?" Nadia said, also standing, responding before Tanya could.

"Yes, we got worried for a minute." Dustin said, smiling down at Nadia. His gray eyes sparkled as the sunlight hit the side of his face.

"Well, time flies when you're having fun." Tanya exclaimed. Reaching her arms up around Ethan's neck and pulling him in for a kiss.

"Well, with a greeting like that, I just might forgive you." Tanya swatted Ethan's chest after his response.

"I'm giving Anita a night off, so we were thinking of ordering some food for dinner. Any suggestions?" Dustin asked. Tanya and Nadia both said 'Chinese'. Nadia looked over at Tanya, who instantly started laughing, causing Nadia and then both Dustin and Ethan to laugh as well.

"Two peas in a pod for sure." Ethan said. Dustin took Nadia's hand and entwined their fingers. Nadia looked up at him and smiled coyly. Ethan placed his arm around Tanya's neck as she, in turn, placed hers around his waist, and the four of them began walking back to the house.

Lyanne Franklin placed her bag on the chair in her study as she walked over to the bar and fixed herself a drink. Moments like this, she truly appreciated the competent staff she'd hired. The bar was fully stocked, and perfectly sized ice cubes were in the ice chest. She poured an ample amount of amber liquid into her glass, added four ice cubes exactly, and took a nice swig.

"Rough day?" A smooth southern voice asked. Lyanne finished her drink before turning and noticing her brother-in-law sitting in the lounger across from the bar.

"That nephew of yours is driving me crazy." She stated, pouring herself another drink, and taking a seat on the sofa, next to the chair that held her purse.

"What's distracting him now?"

"Margery." Lyanne answered dryly. The very thought of Kyle continuing this silly infatuation with Margery just burned her.

"You can't control him, Lyanne, and he's not Khalil." Lyanne sighed at the mention of her eldest son. Taking another strong gulp, she allowed her thoughts to drift to what could have been. How different things might have been if he'd lived. Kyle was always reckless, selfish and could never see beyond his own needs, But Khalil, her first born, was perfect. There was nothing he wouldn't do for her. Nothing he wouldn't do to please her. He was nothing like Kyle or her deceased husband. God rest his soul.

"He's going to throw everything I've built away."

"It's not the life he wants, Lyanne. I've tried to tell you that." His voice was laced with sympathy that she honestly didn't want to hear.

"There's too much time invested just to give up and walk away. Kyle's numbers are dropping by the second." She kicked off her heels, showing no interest in where they landed and took another drink from her glass. The slight burn only lasted a moment, but the rich deep substance calmed her nerves and allowed her to escape for a minute. She leaned her head back on the sofa and closed her eyes. She felt his presence, despite never hearing him move. Her foot was lifted and placed in his lap. She began to moan slowly as she felt his strong hands massage her feet. Finally lifting her head and opening her eyes, she saw he'd slid the footrest over, sitting on it to face her while continuing to massage her feet.

"What do you want to do?"

"I don't know. So much is riding on this, and Kyle has always been a loose cannon. Not to mention the fact that Nadia is in San Antonio with her husband." She took another sip of her drink, loving the feeling of his hands now working up her ankles to her calves.

"If you accept Margery for Kyle, the Senate is still in the bag. She comes from a pretty good family. It wouldn't be the worse option." Leonard stated, still working her calves. She eyed him quizzingly, knowing that Margery could step right in, whip Kyle into shape and save face after the disastrous wedding. The issue was, she just didn't like Margery.

"Maybe, it's not the worst option, but Kyle isn't my main concern right now." Lyanne said, finishing her drink and placing her glass on the side table.

"Tell me what ails you, and I'll do what I can." She smiled at him. He always cured what ailed her, troubled her, and haunted her. This situation even he did not know of.

"It can wait until later." She said, gently sliding her leg from his lap. A knowing smile appeared on his face. She rose, standing in front of him, and began to unbutton her blouse. Her sharp intake of breath echoed through the study as the hands that were once on her calves slowly rose underneath her skirt.

"I will never understand how you can eat that." Dustin heard Ethan say.

"I thought I was the only one who liked to eat egg rolls with ranch instead of duck sauce." Nadia said, taking another bite of her eggroll after dipping it in the ranch.

"Nope, and I'm the genius who introduced you to it." Tanya happily boasted.

"That's just disgusting." Ethan said, shaking his head.

"What about you, Dustin? You want to try it." Tanya offered.

"I think I'll pass." Dustin declined, finishing the last of his Szechuan chicken.

"You can't knock it until you try it." Nadia suggested to Dustin.

"Yes, you can, and I'm telling you to save your taste buds and don't do it." Ethan warned.

"You're over-exaggerating again, Ethan. It's not that bad." Tanya defended.

"I'm actually full, so I'm good." Dustin said, getting up to throw his plate in the sink. After the rest of them finished eating and teasing about the food, they retreated to the family room in the back of the house. Dustin rarely came into this room. It held a lot of items that were special to him. Things belonging to his mom, his grandfather and a couple of gifts from Tricia.

"Oh my gosh! Dustin, I can't believe you still have this." Tanya exclaimed, walking over to the glass-covered cabinet that held his glass horses and figurines collection. He knew the exact one she was referring to.

"I remember the Christmas Tricia gave this to you." Ethan said. Dustin almost stiffened when he felt Nadia stand beside him, but she smiled when he looked down at her.

"I gave that to you?" she asked.

"Yes." He responded as she marveled at the glass horse figurine.

"It's beautiful."

"It is." Dustin smiled down at Nadia. He liked she was willing to learn more about their relationship. The last week had been hard, practically tiptoeing around what to say and what not to. He cherished so many memories with Tricia, Tanya, and Ethan. He was amazed at how much he'd forgotten about. A slight twinge of guilt settled in him for not keeping in touch with them. After returning from Mexico and hearing of Tricia's death, he'd done all he could to keep his sanity. Shortly after, his father had gotten sick, and he diverted most of his attention to taking care of him. Ensuring he was at his side until he took his last breath. He'd lost so much in such a short time. If it hadn't been for Tricia, he probably wouldn't have even gone to college. He'd considered joining the army as Ethan had. But with his dad being sick, he chose a local college, even considered becoming a veterinarian. That had been Tricia's dream, and although he loved animals, especially horses, he wasn't as smart as Tricia was in that field. He graduated with an engineering degree. Dustin loved gadgets, curious about how they worked, what made them function and discovering their distinctive qualities.

"So, what have you been doing with yourself these last few years?" Tanya asked Nadia, bringing him back to the present. Tanya and Ethan sat on one sofa in the family room. He chose a love seat next to them, and surprisingly Nadia came and sat next to him. He rested his arm on the back of the couch, listening to Nadia recall all that happened in her life since she'd woke up in a medical center. A sudden twinge of guilt hit Dustin's chest. He had no logical reason to believe she wasn't dead, but a part of him felt as though he should have looked for her.

"Well, I'm happy you were safe, and everything still worked out okay." Tanya said. Nadia eventually finished telling them how she went to community college, received her associate degree in human resources, volunteered at the children's hospital, and ended up working at Gateway.

Chapter Twelve

Nadia hugged Tanya and Ethan goodbye and watched as they drove away in their SUV. Dustin stood next to her, his hand on her waist, waving goodbye. She truly enjoyed the weekend with them. She and Tanya spent some alone time catching up, and she began to understand why she'd befriended her in the past. Nadia shook with amazement at the many stories she told her of the infamous Tricia Hanson. Apparently making a name for herself, not only during summer camp but also in private school. Her behavior was more discreet at school but just as rambunctious. Dustin's foreman Harper approached them, breaking her thoughts and view of the SUV leaving the gate.

"We're having issues with the grayling on the east end again." Harper said.

"Is he loose?" Dustin asked.

"Yes, jump the fence and is now running in the pastures." Nadia watched Dustin rub his hand down his face.

"I'll be right there." Harper nodded and headed towards the stable.

"I have to go retrieve a horse. Will you be alright for a couple of hours?"

"Sure, but is everything alright? I thought all the horses at the Equestrian were pretty mild-mannered."

"They are. This one isn't a part of the Equestrian. He's one of my personal horses." Nadia nodded in understanding.

"Sounds like a troublemaker." She said. She hadn't visited his personal stable yet. Honestly, the horses made her nervous. They were so big and powerful.

"Not really. He just gets a little antsy at times." He reached for his hat on the rocking chair on the porch and placed it on his head. "Can you ask Ms. Anita to have the boys raise the shutters on the house and the stable? It will probably rain tonight." She looked up and didn't see a cloud in the sky.

"Are you sure?"

"Yes, I'm pretty sure."

"Okay, I'll tell her."

"Thank you. I'll see you later." He leaned down, quickly pecked her cheek and headed off the porch. Turning, she went into the house and found Ms. Anita in the kitchen.

"Good afternoon Ms. Anita."

"Hello, dear." She said, pinching the edge of the dough in the silver pan she was using to make a pie. Nadia relayed the message from Dustin, which she gladly said she'd do.

"Do you need any help?" Nadia asked. Honestly, she had nothing to do. The few books she'd brought with her, she'd read, and she didn't feel like doodling on her notepad.

"Have you ever made a blueberry pie before?" Ms. Anita asked. Nadia shook her head.

"Well, I have about three more pie crust shells I need to make. Do you think you can pinch?"

"I think so."

"Alright." Nadia watched and mimicked everything Ms. Anita showed her. Her hands had never been so sticky and gooey, but she enjoyed the time with the older woman. Ms. Anita was about an inch shorter than her 5 '5 height. She seemed fragile but her hands were strong, Nadia noticed as she kneaded the dough used to make the pies.

"These boys around here just love my blueberry pies." She announced with pride while placing them in the oven. They chatted a while, waiting on the pies to cook.

"So, how are you enjoying your stay?" Ms. Anita asked.

"It's nice. More than nice. Everyone has been so friendly, and I'm just amazed at what Dustin has done here.

"He's a great young man."

"He is." Nadia agreed, thinking of just how amazing he was. "He mentioned you came here because of the Equestrian."

"I did. A little over two years ago."

"What brought you here?" Ms. Anita glanced down into her lap before connecting her eyes back to Nadia's.

"I came here to die." Nadia's eyes widen in dismay.

"What? Why?" Nadia listened as Anita explained how a rare bone disease was discovered in her body thirty years ago. She'd spent over twenty-five years like a lab rat, trying various types of treatments and experimental testing. The last experiment nearly killed her, and she decided to accept her fate and spend whatever time she had left on this earth doing things she'd never done. Riding a horse had been one of them, and she believed fate led her to the Equestrian.

"After being here, almost six months, I started feeling better and scared to death. I've always heard you feel your absolute best right before you die. So, I believed this was the end."

"But it wasn't." Nadia said, completely immersed in Ms. Anita's story.

"No, it was not. I decided to go to what I figured was my last checkup, and low and behold, after running a few tests, they couldn't find anything wrong with me."

"That's amazing, and you are truly a miracle, Ms. Anita."

"Thank you, my dear."

"So, did you do all the things on your bucket list?"

"I have, except for one thing." A sadness seemed to cloud over Ms. Anita. Nadia wanted to ask her what the one thing was she had yet to do. The oven timer chimed, indicating the pies were ready, stifling Nadia's courage to ask. Nadia assisted her in retrieving the pies from the oven. She would be the first to admit they smelled heavenly. Ms. Anita happily chatted, and Nadia listened, laughed with her, still curious about the one thing left on her bucket list.

Dillon closed the door to Donnell's condo, stepped into the living space and dropped the pizza boxes in his arms on the table.

"Took you long enough," Dexter grunted.

"I told you guys to have it delivered." He said, placing the bag of drinks beside the pizzas on the table.

"We were trying to be nice and wait for you." Damien added. His feet propped on the other end of the table while he texted on his phone.

"Where's Donnie? I thought you'd have the card game flowing by now."

"He stepped off into his office for a second." Dexter answered, placing a slice of veggie pizza in his mouth.

"I'll let him know I'm here." Normally Dillon would holler from the living area, but if Donnie were in his office, he might be on the phone. Taking the few steps down the hall, he saw the office door slightly ajar. He heard a little noise, only the clicking of a mouse.

"Knock, Knock." He said, announcing his presence and standing in the doorway.

"Hey. Glad you could make it." Donnie said, not looking up. His eyes were glued to his computer screens.

"Are you working on another case?"

"No, this is actually some more information sent to me on Tricia, or Nadia, I should say.

"Bad news?"

"Just...puzzling." Dillon didn't like the sound of that. Puzzling for most people meant slight confusion or a simple fix. For Donnell, it could lead to a wormhole opening up into an abyss. Dillon walked into the room and took a seat in front of the desk.

"What did you find?" Donnell finally looked up at him and rested back in his chair.

"The medical records and notes were finally sent to me. I'm comparing them to the police reports."

"And?"

"Tricia's parents never identified her body." Donnell answered.

"What? How did they know it was her in the car then?" Dillon asked, now sitting on the edge of his seat.

"The vehicle and her Id, I'm assuming. I'm still waiting on some information."

"Are you sure Nadia is actually Tricia Hanson?"

"Yes. I checked Nadia's dental records against Tricia's old ones, compared a DNA sample based on her drug test from Gateway and verified the birthmark on her upper right thigh."

"So, I guess now you're trying to figure out what caused the accident?

"For the most part, I know. It's just a little taxing because the accident was so long ago." Donnell leaned forward, reading something on his computer.

"Okay, well, take a break. Let's get this card game going."

"Alright." He stood with Dillon and walked over to the door.

"Wait. If you have most of the information on the accident, what information are you waiting on?"

"The person who was in her car."

Dustin stilled his horse as he approached the east end of his property with Harper. The charcoal horse was running back and forth, enjoying the sun shining and the wind drifting through his mane. Everyone needed a moment to let loose and be wild and free. Of course, this horse seemed to like it more than others. His staff suggested several times to heighten the horse corral fence, but Dustin couldn't do it. This horse wasn't like his other breeds.

He hopped down off the brown mare, handing the reins to his foreman.

"Are you sure?" Harper asked.

"Yes. I'll wait until he comes around."

"I sometimes don't understand the patience you have with that horse." Dustin
smiled and watched as Harper turned on his horse and led the other one away. Finding a stump to sit on, Dustin watched the charcoal horse gallop back and forth, eventually stopping. Birds

flew over as the horse extended its neck as if he wished to fly with them. Dustin understood that longing. The air seemed to have more freedom than being on the ground. It was one thing he loved most about flying his helicopter. The freedom in it. No confinements or boundaries. And the solidarity of it was indescribable. Dustin was so lost in thought he hadn't realized the horse spotted him and was now running toward him. He wondered for a moment if he wouldn't stop and run him down. It wouldn't have been the first time. It took him years to find him and the horse's stubbornness caused Dustin to isolate him from the others. Building him his own corral outside his stable. Allowing him the freedom to adjust to his new living area. None of his other horses had that luxury, and it definitely made it hard to keep him confined the first three years. Now they fell into a rhythm, and Dustin began to notice a pattern. Every time a thunderstorm would brew, the horse would get frantic and need to run and thrash about. The horse didn't like thunderstorms. One vet Dustin had on staff noticed it before him. Sure enough, every time he jumped over his fence and began racing to the east area on his property, the rainfall began a few hours later. The horse slowed to a trot before standing in front of him. Dustin slowly stood as the horse made his final steps approaching him. He didn't move a muscle until he was sure the horse was steady. Extending his hand out, his palm flat up, he waited as the horse bowed its head to place it against his palm. Dustin smiled and lightly scratched the horse's head.

"Hey, Puck." He whispered.

"I can't believe I'm actually going to do this." Nadia exclaimed while Dustin was settling the reins in the horse's mouth.

"I told you I'd get you on a horse before your time was up." Yes, he did tell her that and honestly, she'd been nervous about it ever since he mentioned it. It was around six in the morning. Dustin was an early riser, and Nadia was also, so she didn't mind.

"So, how exactly am I going to get on the horse?" Before the words were fully out of her mouth, she heard movement behind her and turned to see Harper holding a stepping stool.

"After you, my lady." Dustin said, stretching his hand out to hers once Harper placed the stepping stool in front of her. She took a deep breath, took Dustin's hand, and allowed both him and Harper to help her mount. The horse moved slightly, and Nadia almost panicked.

"Oh no, please don't move yet. I'm not ready." She chanted, closing her eyes.

"Try and relax." Dustin said as he swiftly and quite easily mounted the horse and sat behind her. She tried to turn her head to look at him in shock but thought better of it when she feared turning too hard would make her fall off the horse. Harper handed Dustin the reins, and with a slight kick of his legs, they began a slow trot. Nadia sat stiffly for the first few minutes of the ride.

"You need to relax. She can sense your nerves. If you're nervous, she'll be nervous." Nadia tried to calm herself as best she could. The last thing she wanted was the horse to sense her nerves and buck, standing on her hind legs knocking both her and Dustin to the ground. She tried to keep her eyes focused on where Dustin was taking her. The vast amount of land he owed confused her about which side of the property they were on.

"It also helps if you move with the horse, it feels funny at first, but it will help slightly with the soreness later."

"Soreness?" She questioned. He hadn't mentioned being sore. She heard Dustin chuckle behind her.

"It's not too uncommon after riding a horse for the first time that muscles you didn't know you had will ache."

"And you didn't think to tell me this before I got on the horse." she said teasingly. She could feel his smile against the side of her face despite not seeing it.

"I didn't want to risk you not agreeing to get on. Plus, I'm hoping once we reach our destination, you'll feel it was worth it."

"Where exactly are you taking me?"

"You'll see." That was the only response she received. She remained quiet the rest of the ride and took in his land site. She heard birds flying overhead, crickets chirping, and even the slight gust of the wind blowing past. It seemed they were approaching a pond or lake. Dustin brought the horse to a stop, and Nadia frowned. They had not come to the brink of the lake. They were still in open pasture.

"This is where you wanted to bring me?" she questioned.

"Just wait." He answered calmly. Patience wasn't always her strong suit when she was nervous. Waiting for what seemed like forever, the most beautiful scene she'd ever encountered happened. The sun began a slow rise over the pasture. The sun's rays hit the lake, causing a glittering effect, making it sparkle like diamonds. The site mixed with the dew on the grass around the lake created a very remarkable picture, almost as if it were a painting.

"Wow." Nadia exhaled.

"I'd hoped you'd like it." Dustin whispered softly in her ear. She wished she could look at him and show him the gratitude reflecting on her face, but fear of falling kept her posture straight. Instead, she slightly leaned back into him. He placed one of his hands that had been holding the reins around her belly. She closed her eyes and let her head fall on his shoulder. A slight gasp expelled from her mouth as he tightened his hold on her.

"Are you alright? Am I holding you too tight?" she shook her head slowly, taking in the site before her and the man's arms she was in. It took all of her strength not to allow the tears that threatened her eyes to fall. The moment she placed her head on his shoulder, a very familiar feeling overtook her. The dream. The dream that plagued her mind for weeks after she'd seen him at Ashiree's baby shower. This was the feeling, the very sensation of being in his arms, feeling comforted, safe, and loved. She sighed. She was certain this was not the first time she'd been in his arms like this. She could conclude that her dream was actually a memory. It felt too real to be anything else. She wasn't sure how long they stayed there, but eventually, Dustin continued their trot alongside the lake and headed back to the stables. He was right. No matter how sore she felt after, the ride had been worth it. And although the view had been breathtaking, so had being in his arms.

Chapter Thirteen

DUSTIN was thankful for the distraction Harper provided once he and Nadia returned from their ride. He could admit it turned out better than he'd hoped. He loved watching the sunrise. There was something so soothing, calming, and peaceful about it. The first time he'd found the lake and saw how it glittered just as the sun rose, it became his favorite spot on his property. He wanted to share it with Nadia. Hoping she would appreciate the scene. She had, so much so, that she leaned back against him to enjoy the view. He couldn't express how much sharing that experience meant to him, but what he hadn't expected was the intense surge of pleasure that vibrated through his body the moment she laid her head on his shoulder. The melancholy emotion was not foreign, but it was missed. He recalled several moments where he and Tricia sat by the bank of the lake at camp, and she leaned against him just as Nadia had today. It was hard separating them at times. So many little things kept his mind and heart at odds. His mind was very much aware of the woman he fell in love with as a teenage boy and stayed in love with well into his adulthood, which differed completely from the woman with him now. But his heart responded as if it knew her, no matter the time, no matter her memory, and no matter where they were.

"Some sensors along the fences alongside the Equestrian are misreading." Harper said, bringing Dustin out of his thoughts as they headed to the Equestrian. The walk wasn't far, but they chose to take a golf cart.

"I need to adjust the sensitivity. Plenty of the patrons like to lean against the fences, and that shouldn't cause the sensors to misfire or short out." Harper nodded at his words but didn't speak. Dustin liked that about Harper. He was a man of few words. After checking the sensor and replacing it, Dustin headed back toward the house. Once he made it in, he took the stairs two at a time and headed to the room at the end of the hall. He kept the door shut but rarely locked it. There weren't many people in his home besides Ms. Anita and now Nadia. Opening the door, which creaked slightly, he turned on the light and walked over to the table housing the sensors for the fences. Opening a small black box on the side of the table, he placed the misfiring sensor in it and turned on his laptop.

"Knock, knock." he heard. Turning around, he saw Nadia standing in the doorway.

"Hey."

"Hi. Can I come in?" She asked.

"Sure." He said while motioning his arm. He grabbed a chair from out of the corner of the room.

"Have a seat." He suggested. She slowly looked around as she entered the room, and he wondered what she thought of it for a minute. To most, it might have looked like a junk room for old appliances, but to him, it was his pastime when he wasn't working around the farm. Taking things apart, putting them back together, finding out how they worked, seeing if he could improve them. That's what he liked.

"What is all this?" She asked, taking a seat.

"My secret hideaway." He said jokingly when turning back to his computer.

"I see." He heard her say and was pretty sure she was still looking around, confused.

"What's this?" she asked, pointing at the moving graphs on his computer."

"This is an error detection scale." He answered, then looked down at her and noticed her brows raised. He explained further. Showing her the different spikes, showing the test he was running on the misfiring sensor. He also explained how they were placed along the entire surrounding area on his property. Alerting him if anyone entered his property without his or Harper's knowledge.

"You created all this." He nodded.

"So, this is what you meant when you said you were into gadgets?"

"Pretty much." He responded.

"So, is it like an invisible force field?" She asked. He chuckled at her question.

"It doesn't zap people if that's what you mean, but it does send an electric pulse to ward off other animals from the farm.

"Does it hurt them?"

"No. It's kind of like a dog whistle, but instead of calling the animals to it, it drives animals away from it.

"That's kind of cool. How did you come up with it?"

"Honestly, by accident." he said, typing something on his laptop to see where he could fix the issue in the sensor.

"How?"

"Well, I hired a company to do some fencing when I first received the property. I knew what I wanted to do with the land, but getting everything up and running took a while. I was constantly calling the company because the fence lines kept signaling an intruder."

"Was there one?" Nadia asked.

"No. But I took some linings being replaced and examined them. I was curious to know exactly how it worked. I ended up in here for almost fourteen hours and eventually created my own sensor. The dog whistle was added later. I'm still working the kinks out on that one.

"Wow. I'm impressed." She said. Looking over at her, his breath caught in his chest. Those brown eyes, full of excitement, those lips beckoning for a kiss, and her scent wrapping its way around his nostrils, causing his libido to spike. A ping from his laptop brought his attention back to the sensors, showing what was causing the misfire.

"Does that tell you what is wrong?" She asked, pointing to the diagram displayed on the laptop, flashing red on the model of the sensor.

"Yes." He responded, studying the diagram a little harder than needed to gain some control over his attraction to her.

"Well, I'll let you get to that and grab something to eat from the kitchen." She said as she stood.

"This will only take a second." He assured her.

"No rush." She stated, placing the chair back in the corner from where she saw him grab it for her earlier.

"Nadia." He called out before she was fully out of the room. "Have you been to San Antonio's Riverwalk?"

"Not that I remember." She answered playfully, and he couldn't help but chuckle.

"I was thinking we could go later."

"Sure, I'd like that."

"Good, be ready in about an hour."

'Okay." She said, practically beaming at his invitation. He watched her walk out of the room and noticed the subtle sway of her hips. He ran a hand down his face. Getting out of the house would be a good idea. Between the feeling of her in his arms during their ride and the scent of her delicate perfume, he was afraid he might not contain himself much longer being alone with her.

"I thought you left." Kyle said, rubbing his eyes while entering his living room. Margery was on his couch looking at an old photo album. She looked up and smiled at him.

"You were sleeping so soundly I didn't want to wake you." She answered.

"I don't like waking up, and you're not next to me." Kyle said, plopping down on the couch next to her. He leaned over and kissed her lips.

"You say the sweetest things. You know that." Margery smiled against his lips, still feeling as if this wasn't real. Being with Kyle this week had been amazing. She gave up on her feelings for him almost four years ago when it was obvious Lyanne Franklin did not approve of her. If she were honest, she didn't care for Lyanne herself. But she wanted Kyle to succeed. He would make a wonderful Senator, and she supported that, even to the extent of never being the woman at his side. But it seems luck might be on her side. She guessed she should thank a very wealthy cowboy for her current happiness. She had nothing against Nadia, they were opposites in almost every way, but she secretly prayed Nadia would stay with her husband in San Antonio.

"What are you looking at?" Kyle asked, interrupting her thoughts.

"One of your old photo albums, it was stuffed in this couch." Margery replied as Kyle looked down at the pictures. He slightly stiffened.

"What's wrong?" Margery asked, feeling the slight tension as Kyle ran a finger over one picture.

"This isn't mine. It's my brother Khalil's."

"I didn't know you had a brother."

"He died a long time ago." Kyle tried to smile as he answered Margery. He'd remembered his brother being there, then it felt like the next moment, he was gone.

"I'm sorry, Kyle."

"It's alright." he said absentmindedly, looking at more pictures. As Margery continued to flip the pages, Kyle laughed at a few, as he and his brother did silly poses and funny faces at the camera.

"You guys look really happy."

"He was my best friend growing up."

"How did he die?"

"His heart gave out." Kyle answered.

"I'm sure that was hard on both of you." Kyle nodded, not wanting to say anything else about his brother. He didn't talk about him to anyone. Not even his mother.

"Hey, when was this?" Margery asked, looking at a picture of Khalil in a suit.

"Probably one of the debutante balls my mom made him escort in."

"Who's the girl?" Kyle took the photo out to get a better look. There was a strong resemblance to the girl in the photo. It only took a few seconds for his brain to make the connection. Margery's phone vibrated on the table next to him, and she leaned over to answer it before he could answer her question. He placed the photo back in the album and asked Margery if she wanted something to eat. She nodded, and he stood, taking the album with him to his room and grabbed his own phone. After placing an order to have the food delivered, he sat on his bed and opened the album to the photo again. Curiosity and confusion gripped his thoughts. The photo displayed a younger version of Nadia, or more so the young woman Tricia Hanson. How had they known each other? A disturbing thought entered his mind. If Khalil knew Tricia Hanson, it was likely his mother also did. Pondering on that thought, he suspected his mother also knew Tricia Hanson and Nadia Bolton, were one and the same.

Nadia couldn't remove the smile from her face as she and Dustin walked the many shops in the Riverwalk. She wasn't big on shopping, or at least she hadn't thought she was. Currently, she had three gift bags worth of items. Just a few trinkets to remember her time in San Antonio. She and Dustin paused from walking from store to store when a group of street performers began their routine. She laughed, clapped, and moved her head to the beat. Dustin suggested they eat. They soon sat at a nice cafe alongside the river. Nadia watched as boats passed by as a waitress left after taking their order. She only had three more days until her mini-vacation was over. She didn't want to leave if she were honest with herself, which surprised her.

"Are you enjoying yourself?" Dustin asked her, interrupting her thoughts.

"Yes." She smiled at him, then looked back over at the boats passing by.

"Would you like to take a boat ride after this?"

"If you wouldn't mind." She answered, trying to calm down her enthusiasm.

"Not at all." He responded. The waitress brought their food over, and Nadia saw a little boy run past with a cowboy hat on and a tiny horse in his hand. His mother was trying desperately to keep up with him. Seeing the little horse reminded her of something she wanted to ask Dustin. She waited for him to finish blessing his food before she spoke.

"I have a question for you."

"You can ask me anything." Dustin said.

"The name of the Equestrian is Maribel's...How did you come up with that?" She watched Dustin finish chewing before he answered.

"Maribel is my mother's name." He answered solemnly. She caught the flash of sorrow in his eyes before he returned to eating.

"Can you tell me about her?" She asked shyly, feeling very selfish at that moment. She had not thought to ask before now. She'd been so wrapped up in finding out about the life she once had. She knew little about him outside of the farm, the Equestrian, and his fascination with gadgets. She had been with him for over a week and hadn't thought to ask about his family. She knew of his brothers from what Margery told her and that his father was now deceased, along with his mother, but what about other relatives or family still in Mexico?

"Sure." He stated, surprised that she asked. Nadia tried to keep the guilt inside her at bay. "She was a nurse." He continued. "She worked in the emergency department. That's how she met my father. He was hurt during a bombing of a construction site for a new resort." Nadia's eyes widened hearing his words. He continued telling the story of his parents, how his father lived with them during his recovery and the decision for him to come live with his father when he was ten.

"Did you not want to live with your father?" She asked.

"A part of me did. I didn't see him often. I didn't understand why he couldn't stay with us, but my mother's decision was ultimately based on two things. "

"What were they?"

"My safety and her breast cancer."

"Why?"

"She didn't want me to see her suffer or slowly slip away, and it seemed the best option.

"I can understand her not wanting you to see her slowly dying, but why did you need to be protected?"

"A few local boys followed me home from school one day and jumped me. Beat me up pretty bad, called me names like bastard or mixed breed. Most of the people from our town knew my father was white and that my parents weren't married."

"That must have been hard."

"Not at first. I had a few friends and chose to focus on them. But it was harder moving here."

"Because of your brothers?"

"Yes, but not just them. People here did not restrain in expressing their concerns for my father welcoming his illegitimate son into his home. It also didn't sit well that he did it a week after burying his wife.

"I can see that causing a little scandal."

"Try a big scandal, but my father never treated me differently. He was proud to have me in his home, to have me in his life. That was enough for me to ignore everyone else's issues or opinions of our family."

"What about your brothers?"

"Jacob was always a little more self-absorbed, and he's older than me by four years, so he practically ignored me most of the time. Matthew was a different story. He tried to make my life a living hell. And the more my father scolded him for it, the more he hated me.

"I heard about the lawsuit." She admitted.

"That was the ugliest thing I've ever been through. I never knew how much Matthew truly despised me until the reading of the Will."

"Did he feel you received more than him?" Nadia asked.

"Hardly. I didn't understand the true extent of my father's wealth or the wealth of his family as a whole. To be honest, I got the short end of the stick. Sure, it's a massive amount of money for a guy like me, but I was only bequeathed what my father actually built for himself. The wealth of his father, and that of Jacob and Matthew's mother, far surpassed anything I received. Matthew just hated that I received anything." She could see the strain in his neck as he talked about the situation with his brothers.

"What about your grandparents? Are they still alive?"

"My dad's parents, no. They both died before even Jacob was born. My mother's mom is deceased also, but her father, my *abuelo*, is very much alive. I go to see him twice a year. He doesn't like me to visit too often. It makes him feel like I'm doting on him, and he's a very proud man."

"I'm happy you still have him."

"So am I." They finished the last of their food, and Dustin tipped the waitress.

"How about that boat ride?" He suggested, those gray eyes sparkling in the sunlight.

"I'd love to."

Chapter Fourteen

Donnell walked into the simple office building, headed toward the elevator, and pushed the button for the fifteenth floor. He watched as the exchange of others entered and exited the elevator, smiled, and talked cheerfully, while some huffed annoyances about it only being Wednesday. Arriving at the destination floor, he took his badge out, following the necessary procedures in retina scan and fingerprint verification of identity. Two guards escorted him to the office of the man he came to visit.

"Mason. What do I owe this pleasure?" the man said, greeting him by his last name and dismissing the guards who closed the door as Donnell took a seat.

"I need you to look at something." He answered, pulling an envelope out of the inside of his jacket pocket and handing it across the table.

"Must be pretty important if you decided to come in person." the man responded, taking the envelope from him.

"It's just a hunch." the man huffed, fully aware of the contradiction a hunch was for Donnell. As he waited for the man to read his report, he glanced around. The one window in the office faced another office building, the lighting was poor, but the office was hardly used. Only for meetings like this, only as a disguise to hide the things truly going on in the world. The man put the paper and envelope down on the table, intertwined his fingers and rested back in his chair.

"How big is this hunch?" The man questioned.

"Proof or gut?" Donnell asked.

"Both?"

"Proof? Maybe ten percent, gut? closer to ninety."

"How did you stumble on to this?"

"Looking up background information on one of my friend's wives."

"Again?? What the heck kind of women are your friends involved with? First, you give Austin some stolen drug tip, resulting in them discovering a dead body. And those jerks in LA are still upset they can't take credit for the arrest at LAX. Then, that club in San Antonio uncovered a sex trafficking ring, not to mention that lawyer in Tennessee is still contacting me, and now this!" Donnell huffed out a breath. He'd stepped on a few toes this last year with the situation surrounding his friends. He wouldn't feel bad about it. He hadn't been looking for these occurrences. They just happen to stumble in his lap. He liked puzzles, and it was hard to stop once he got started.

"What do you need from me? Because I know it is not my permission to continue down this rabbit hole." Donnell tried not to smirk. He rarely asked for permission.

"I need a tail." He heard the man behind the desk groan.

"For how long?"

"Maybe a couple of weeks tops."

"I'll have Flynn at your doorstep in two days."

"We both know Archer is best."

"Archer is AWAL."

"Still?"

"Don't worry, I know where he is, and we're keeping slight tabs on him."

"It's been two years."

"Some need more time than others. How's Sean doing?"

"Pretty well, Dominic's pleased." Donnell answered. Silence hung between them for a moment.

"I don't need to warn you how bad this could go if you're wrong."

"I just need a few days. If I can't find what I need, I'll back off."

"Yeah, I'll believe that when I see it. Good luck, my friend." They both stood and shook hands. Donnell exited the room as the man took a lighter to the paper and tossed it in the wastebasket.

Dustin placed a sleeping Nadia in the bedroom she was occupying in his home. The thought of laying her down in his bed crossed his mind, but he'd thought better of it. He didn't want to frighten her. Gently pulling the blanket over her, he took a minute to look at her as she peacefully slept. Today had gone well, better than he could have imagined. They talked, laughed, and lightly flirted. After eating, he took her on the riverboat ride. Other couples surrounded them, kids squirming in their seats and crying babies. None of that mattered. He was happy to enjoy the feel of her in his arms. As they took in the scene floating along the river, he could feel the steady beating of her heart as she rested her head on the lower part of his shoulder. Conflicting emotions constantly plagued him. That had been Tricia's favorite thing to do as well. He fought several memories of the times they were together, at the camp, by the lake, even the few times she snuck away, using Tanya as a cover with her parents to go to the drive-in with him. But this wasn't Tricia. It was Nadia. That was hard to continue to tell his heart. After their boat ride, she seemed tired, so they headed back to his ranch. The drive was an hour away, and he'd rented a car and driver to enjoy relaxing and being with her. She'd fallen asleep, no doubt due to all the walking they'd done. He'd tried to wake her, but just as Tricia had been quite the heavy sleeper, so was Nadia.

Breathing out a sigh, he left her in the room and closed the door softly. He entered his bedroom. It was twice the size of the living room downstairs, allowing for not only a California king-size bed, along with his dresser and chest, but a sitting space in front of a brick fireplace. He'd also built a balcony right off the master bedroom, allowing him to enjoy any sunrise whenever he didn't walk with Puck to the lake. The connecting bathroom was the size of the room Nadia was currently sleeping in. A full wall vanity with mirrors and lights went the length of the wall opposite his bedroom. It was the one thing he'd let an interior designer talk him into while building the house. A double head shower stall was completely glassed-in, and the step-up massive jacuzzi tub took up the far corner. He'd never used the tub. He wasn't an avid bath person. However, he remembered Tricia had been. And just like most of the things he'd done over the last eight years on the property, he had her in mind. Hitting the remote on the side of the wall to turn on the shower, he stripped, wondering if Nadia liked baths as Tricia had. He never had a woman in his bathroom. When he decided to share company with a woman, he never brought her to his home. He hadn't been with many women but letting another woman in his space or in his heart seemed impossible.

Stepping into the shower, he allowed the warm water to run over his head and cascade down his body. Thoughts of Nadia at the forefront of his mind conflicted with thoughts of Tricia. How could he separate the two? Did he have to choose? Was it fair to Nadia to want everything he'd had with Tricia? Was it unfair to Tricia's memory to embrace his growing feelings and attraction for Nadia? In all truth, they were the same woman, but only physically. Mentally and emotionally, they were completely different. The fact was, he wanted both, was attracted to both, and dare he say, loved both, placing a constant war between his heart and his mind. It didn't matter if she regained her memory or not. He'd always want her. Remembering Dominic's words, he smiled, feeling confident that maybe, he could get her to fall in love with him all over again.

Nadia walked into the kitchen with an extra pep in her step. Ms. Anita was cooking bacon that filled the house with the most welcoming aroma.

"Good morning Ms. Anita."

"Good morning Nadia. Did you sleep well?"

"I did." She answered with a whimsical smile on her face. Yesterday with Dustin had been just what she needed to feel closer to him. After they talked more about his grandfather and then the boat ride, she'd felt more in tune with him. Sneaking glances at him when he wasn't looking, subtle touches of their hands, and him standing so close to her she could feel his breath on her neck when he spoke. The car ride home, she'd fallen asleep, leaning on his shoulders, and had awakened in her bed. Knowing Dustin must have carried her, she sighed. She would have been complete putty in his arms if she had been awake. And he was a gentleman. She was sure had it been any other man. She probably would have awakened in his bed.

"Nadia." She blinked out of her thoughts, realizing Ms. Anita had called her name.

"I'm sorry, I didn't hear you." Ms. Anita smiled knowingly at her, and Nadia blushed.

"It seems something, or maybe someone is occupying those thoughts of yours." Nadia blushed again, not even trying to hide it.

"Yes, guilty as charged." She admitted.

"Young love. It truly is a blessing."

"Have you ever been in love?" She watched Ms. Anita place the cooked bacon on a tray and begin cracking eggs.

"I can say I was, once."

"Really?" Nadia said curiously, taking a seat at the table in the nook area.

"Yes, and we were married for almost fifteen years. "

"Wow, that's a pretty long time." Ms. Anita shrugged.

"It was common in my day. You got married young, had children, and lived happily ever after." she said with a sad smile as she cooked the eggs.

"Did the two of you have children together?" Ms. Anita shook her head.

"God didn't see fit that I have children with my Bruce." Ms. Anita answered, cutting off the stove and handing Nadia a plate.

"Was that because of your disease?" Nadia asked after she blessed her food and did her best not to moan when biting the perfectly crisp bacon.

"Actually, no. I didn't find out about my disease until my late thirties. Come to find out Bruce actually couldn't produce children."

She answered as she placed a cup of tea on the table for Nadia and a cup of coffee for herself.

"Did you want children?" Nadia asked cautiously. She knew there were women who had no desire to have kids.

"I did. Almost had the opportunity, once." Ms. Anita answered sorrowfully. Nadia didn't know what to say after that. The mournful tone in Ms. Anita's voice made her heartache. She instantly thought about having children herself. She knew if she'd married Kyle, his mother definitely expected her to have a few, creating the image of this perfect family. But listening to Ms. Anita, she wondered if she wanted kids. The idea was pleasant, but she'd spent so much time in her life just trying to make the best out of it with her memory gone. She hadn't really stopped and thought about what she truly wanted.

"I didn't mean to make you sad, child." Ms. Anita said, clearly sensing the uneasiness in Nadia's face.

"I don't know what to say when things get awkward or uncomfortable. I never want to say the wrong thing or make the situation worse.

"It's fine. I've made my peace with it." Nadia nodded and continued eating the rest of her breakfast.

"What do you plan on doing today? I know Dustin is currently out with Harper at the moment." Ms. Anita asked, finishing her coffee.

"Not sure." Nadia answered while shrugging her shoulders. "I've read all the books I've brought. I might doodle a little later."

"I saw you doing something in that notepad the other afternoon. I never really had the artistic ability to create anything."

"I'm not so sure about that. You are very good at creating in the kitchen." Ms. Anita threw her head back and laughed.

"Oh, if my mother could hear you say that. God rest her soul. She kicked me out of her kitchen many times for mixing things around. I set her kitchen on fire a couple of times."

"Oh, no!" Nadia exclaimed.

"Yes. I love mixing things, even wanted to go to school to be a chemist."

"Wow. You're full of surprises, Ms. Anita."

"I could shock you with some of my stories, dear." Nadia laughed at Ms. Anita's intriguing tone.

"Did you ever get a degree in chemistry?"

"I did, actually. After Bruce died, I taught a chemistry class for a few years at a college up north."

"I didn't know you weren't from Texas." Nadia stated, growing more and more curious about Ms. Anita.

"I'm a Massachusetts girl through and through. Grew up only a few blocks away from Paul Revere's house."

"Paul Revere?" Nadia questioned. Ms. Anita's eyes widened in utter dismay.

"You don't know who Paul Revere is?" Nadia shook her head.

"What are they teaching children in the school system today?" Ms. Anita gave a disapproving stare before she continued. "It appears I'll be giving you a history lesson today." Nadia smiled and spent the rest of the morning listening to Ms. Anita's lesson in history.

Dustin stepped onto the back porch. Nadia was sitting on the sofa, with her feet tucked underneath her doodling in her notepad.

"Hey." He said softly as not to startle her.

"Hi." She answered, smiling as she looked up at him.

"You seem pretty engrossed in that sketch."

"It's one that I've sketched many times before." She answered, then scooted over a little so he could sit next to her.

"I guess you like it." Dustin responded. She shrugged her shoulders, looking back down at the sketch.

"I don't know what it is." She admitted.

"Do you mind if I take a look?"

"Sure." she said, handing over the notepad. Dustin looked at the lines. The areas shaded darker in some spots. It didn't look like anything in particular. He squinted his eyes to ensure he wasn't missing any detail but came up short.

"Sorry, I got nothing." He said with a chuckle as he handed it back to her.

"That's alright. I've drawn this many times before and could never figure it out." As she took the sketchpad back from Dustin, she placed her pencil in the spiral rings at the top and began to place it on the table.

"Wait, let me see that again?" Dustin asked, catching a glimpse of the sketch from a different angle. Nadia gave him a questioning look but handed the sketch back to him. Dustin took it and turned it upside down. The darker shaded areas now closer to the bottom of the page, the square-like shapes in the back and the long rectangle figures all began to come together in his mind.

"How long did you say you've been drawing this?" He asked, his breath almost shaking in unbelief. It couldn't be what he thought.

"Since I first started doodling. Maybe a couple of years after I woke up. It was one of the first things I drew. Why? Do you know what it is?" Dustin nodded his head but did not answer immediately. He wasn't even sure how he would tell her what he suspected it was.

"It's a barn." He stated, still astonished that she'd drawn it.

"It doesn't look like a barn. Even turned upside down." she said teasingly. Dustin smirked at her teasing but further explained.

"It's not a whole barn. It's a storage area in a barn."

"A storage area? What does it store?"

"Hay, old tools, nonchalant or forgotten things."

"Wow, that's strange. I wonder why I would draw that?" she said, leaning over more toward the sketch, trying to see what he saw. Dustin handed her back the notepad and slowly stood up. He knew exactly why she'd drawn it, knew what that storage meant to him, or rather to him and Tricia. He walked a couple of steps to the porch railing, placed his hands in his pockets and stared out into the pastures. So many memories flooded his mind of all the times they'd shared, laughing, joking, sneaking around hiding from Brett.

"Dustin?" He heard the concern in Nadia's voice as she called his name. He took a deep breath and turned to face her, resting his back on the beam connected to the railing. Looking at the woman that had his heart. The only woman that had his heart. He tried as hard as he could to separate the two of them, clearly seeing their differences, ready to move forward with Nadia, but there were times like these when Tricia was present. Even unbeknownst to Nadia, she was trying to communicate somehow. Letting him know she hadn't forgotten him completely, that he was just as much in her heart as she was in his, no matter what her mind remembered.

"Does this storage area mean something?" Nadia asked. He nodded, knowing it was still uncomfortable for her to hear memories of them.

"It was our secret spot." He admitted. She slowly nodded in understanding.

"I'm sorry." She said earnestly.

"Don't be. You didn't know."

"That doesn't make it easier." She admitted. None of it was easy. Their secret spot in the barn held a lot of precious memories.

"It doesn't, but it's not something we can control." He said, finally getting his bearings together and coming to sit down beside her again.

"So, did we sneak off here to get stolen kisses or something?" She asked, trying to lighten the mood.

"Yes, I had to pry you off of me."

"Whatever, Dustin." She said, swatting at him. He laughed, grateful for the mood shift.

"Seriously, you were insufferable." He said teasingly.

"Sure, blame it on me since I can't argue because I don't remember." she responded playfully. He liked she could joke about it. It definitely helped in moments like this.

"You weren't that bad, but honestly, we went to the storage area to see all the horses at once. From up there, you could see into every stall. And the overhang was just above Gretel's.

"Who is Gretel?" Nadia asked. Dustin sighed. In just that one question, the mood shifted back again.

Chapter Fifteen

Nadia wrapped a towel around her body as she exited the shower. She used a cloth to wipe the fog from the mirror and took a second to look at herself. Her big brown eyes filled with so many emotions and uncertainties. Lost in her thoughts, she recalled her time with Dustin on the back porch. She'd been able to lighten the mood just a little by mentioning him using the secret spot for stolen kisses, only to be hit with a bombshell when he answered her question of who Gretel was. If she thought it was hard for Dustin to discuss what once was his secret spot with Tricia, it was twice as hard to discuss Gretel. A beautiful black thoroughbred that lived in the stable of the summer camp they visited every year.

Walking into the bedroom, she sat on the bed and picked up a picture from the nightstand. It was the same picture Dustin tried to show her the day of her wedding. She only caught a glimpse of it before Kyle had taken it from her hands. With a full-out war brewing between Kyle and Dustin, she'd fled the room and completely forgotten about the picture. Looking at it now, she saw a much younger version of the both of them, standing next to Gretel. Her face was slightly hidden as she smiled, nuzzling into Gretel. Dustin was all smiles behind her, one hand on Gretel's back and the other wrapped around her. His hair was longer then. Not enough to put in a ponytail, but long enough to run her fingers through it. Completely different from the short, chopped cut he wore now. She laid back on the bed, bringing the picture to her chest. Listening to Dustin earlier explain how he'd lost his mom the same year he lost Gretel, followed by losing her and then his father the next summer, brought pain to her heart she could never explain. She'd been so focused on herself, so focused on Dustin's feelings for someone she no longer was, that she hadn't paid attention to all that he'd suffered. He lost everyone he loved in a short time span. She finally understood the words he'd spoken, about his college days and some girls being a distraction. She couldn't imagine it. She didn't have any memories of her past, and somehow, she felt she was in a better position than Dustin because of it. Could she really handle such a loss? Sighing to herself, she wished she could comfort him. It seemed after he explained everything about their secret spot, his parents and Gretel, he needed some time alone. She only nodded and watched him leave the porch as he headed to what she could only assume would be the lake. She'd picked up her notepad and headed back into the house. She checked on Ms. Anita, asked if she needed anything and went to her room.

About an hour later, she heard Dustin's boots hitting the stairs and closing his bedroom door. Deciding to take a shower, she now wondered if she'd be brave enough to go to him. He playfully joked before about her counterpart being fearless, forthcoming, and never afraid to go after what she wanted. Could she be so brave? Could she conjure up some boldness and go to him? Sitting up, she placed the picture back on the nightstand and went to find her nightgown. It wasn't anything fancy or sexy, just a simple satin beige gown that stopped around her ankles. Quickly finding her bag, she began to lather her body with her vanilla-scented body cream. The anticipation of what she was doing caused heat to rise inside her. She wasn't naïve; she knew exactly what could happen between her and Dustin by going to him. Before she could talk herself out of it or lose her nerve, she slid into her nightgown, snatched off the shower cap she forgot she was wearing and took a deep breath. Opening her bedroom door and stepping out of her room, a tiny squeak in the wooden floors etched louder than normal due to the quietness in the house. Walking over to Dustin's bedroom door, she felt as if her heart was beating a million miles a minute. Conjuring up her last ounce of bravery, she knocked softly on his door. She didn't hear any movement on the other side.

Nadia believed he might have already fallen asleep until he opened the door, and all the bravery she thought she'd conjured up, went out the window. Dustin Shaw was standing before her in a towel. Her eyes slowly drifted from his wet hair to his muscled shoulders, continuing to his flat abs, which still glistened with a few drops of water, down past his towel to his feet. Was it possible for a man to have pretty feet? She heard him clear his throat, and her eyes shot up to his. His gray eyes gleamed with interest, stared back at her. The attraction between them sizzled in the air as she did her best to remember to breathe. Dustin took a step back, opening the door wider to invite her in. She mustered up her last bit of courage, slowly entered his room, and he closed the door behind her.

"So, you're determined to make this thing with Margery, public knowledge, I see." Kyle rolled his eyes as his mother stood in the doorway of his office.

"Yes, Mother." He answered dryly.

"I don't understand why you couldn't just give Nadia a couple of weeks. Once she returns, she'll be back to her old self." Kyle took his glasses off and sat back in his chair.

"And which old self are you referring to, mother? The complacent Nadia? Or the supposedly dead Tricia Hanson?" He watched his mother stiffen for a second. If he hadn't been looking directly at her, he might have missed it.

"I'm not sure what you mean?"

"Oh, I think you do." He said, standing and waving the picture in his hand. "You truly thought you could play me for a fool."

"Kyle, I don't...."

"Cut the BS, mom." He said, walking over to her and handing her the picture. "This picture is of Khalil with Tricia Hanson. All this time, I thought you believed in me, wanted me to make a difference, and now I see you just wanted me to replace the son you lost." He took a few steps back from her and went to his minibar. "Then I began to wonder what's so special about this girl.

Why were you pushing so hard for me to marry her? I also ran into a very interesting person." He continued, pouring himself a drink. "Camille Kerchel. She told me she's been working at Gateway Pharmaceuticals for the last eight months. Coincidently, shortly after Donna Fallon got arrested, you helped her get the job." He paused, taking a sip and watched his mother try to maintain her composure. She was hiding something. Something major and she did not like the fact that he was trying to figure it out. He saw her smile coyly and took a seat on the sofa next to the minibar.

"There's nothing wrong with me helping an old friend's daughter get a job, Kyle." He frowned. He knew his mother better than that. She did nothing without reason, and he would not let this go. For most of his adult life, he tried his best to please her. Knowing the pain of losing her oldest son, her best son, weighed heavily on her. He'd given her grief being the rambunctious teen that he'd been. But after Khalil died, he tried his best to behave. He let her call all the shots in his life, under the assumption that she wanted what was best for him and to keep her fears at bay of losing another son. Now he was pretty sure she just liked calling the shots and being in control of everything.

"You're up to something." He said, pointing a finger at her, with his glass in his hand. "And I'm going to figure it out."

Dustin watched a sleeping Nadia sprawled out under the covers in his bed. She'd come to him last night. A very pleasant surprise and one he welcomed. Their conversation had taken a turn he hadn't expected. The last week, he'd been honest in sharing memories of their past, trying not to hide anything from her while also cautious not to overwhelm her. Discussing Gretel brought emotions out of him he thought he'd dealt with. The last summer at camp had been the hardest summer of his life. He'd lost his mom a few weeks before camp started, then lost both Gretel and Puck by the end of the summer. He hadn't even had the heart to tell Nadia about Puck. He figured at some point he should. However, talking about that summer would lead to discussing losing her and then his father. Feeling overwhelmed, he'd taken a walk and ended up halfway to the lake before turning around. Ms. Anita had already retreated to her room, and Nadia, he assumed, turned in for the night. He was just finishing his shower when he heard the light knock on his bedroom door. Opening his door, he saw Nadia standing before him in an off-white gown that hugged her body in all the right places. Attempting to control himself, he did his best not to gawk at her but immediately noticed her eyes were fixated on everything but his. A slight inch of pride welled inside of him as she openly stared at him from head to toe. Feeling the desire awaking in him, he cleared his throat to get her attention. The brown eyes that connected with his, as her head shot up, realizing she'd been caught, flamed with yearning, an unexplainable longing, and an ache he was all too familiar with. He would not question it, so he took a step back, silently inviting her into his room. No words were spoken, as their bodies communicated what they needed, what they longed for, and what they truly desired.

A slight humming sound interrupted his thoughts. He hurried to the nightstand and retrieved his phone. Picking it up and seeing Donnell was calling, he quietly stepped out onto the balcony to not wake Nadia.

"Hey Donnie," He answered.

"Dustin! How are things going?" Donnell asked. Dustin looked through the glass doors of his balcony at Nadia sleeping and smiled. Things were going great as far as he was concerned.

"Not too bad on this end. What's going on? You're calling pretty early."

"I figured you'd be up, but I wanted to discuss some things I've discovered with Nadia. When is she supposed to be coming back?" Donnell asked. Dustin told him, but he didn't want her to leave if he were honest.

"Let her know it's important."

"I will. Thanks, Donnie." He ended the call and looked out into the pasture as the sunlight began to cascade over his property. The thought of Nadia leaving didn't sit well with him. He wanted her to stay, wanted her to choose him and the life they could have together. Exhaling a short breath, he opened the balcony door to his room. Placing his phone back on the nightstand, he quietly laid in his bed to not wake Nadia. As if on instinct, she reached for him, and he gently pulled her into his embrace. She moaned her appreciation but never awakened. Dustin gently kissed her temple and continued to hold her until sleep took over him again.

Nadia held Dustin's hand as they ascended the stairs to Donnell's apartment. Two days ago, she'd awakened to the best feeling of being in Dustin's arms. The sunlight shone through the blinds of the balcony door, hitting just below Dustin's lips and onto his chin. She wasn't sure how long she stared at him as he slept, but she knew she never wanted to leave that spot. Eventually, he did wake and inform her of his talk with Donnell. Donnell claimed he had some rather important information for her.

Donnell greeted them, opened the door and invited them in. He offered them both some water, which Nadia accepted nervously, and escorted them to his office. The décor in the hallway that led to his office showed various paintings and pictures of different monuments and places around the city of Houston. Nadia especially liked the one showing a bird's-eye view over Houston. It reminded her of when Dustin had flown her around the city in his helicopter.

"You seem nervous?" Dustin said, entering Donnell's office and taking a seat in front of the desk. Donnell sat down behind it. He had a few folders on his desk, two monitors and various stacks of paper.

"I'm not nervous. I just haven't found what I'm truly looking for." Nadia raised her brow at his response.

"But you have some information for me?" She asked.

"Yes." He responded. He looked over at Dustin, who nodded his head in her peripheral, then back at her. Donnell reached for a file folder and handed it to her.

"I'll show you this first." He said as she took the folder from him. She opened it and saw it was an old newspaper article. She narrowed her eyes at the couples in the picture.

"Are these my parents?" She asked. The article's title displayed a medical convention dated over thirty years ago. She glanced at the other couple and noticed something familiar about them.

"Is that Lyanne and Kyle's uncle?" She asked, looking up at Donnell.

"It's actually Lyanne and her late husband Kenneth, Kyle's father."

"They know each other?" She asked. Donnell nodded.

"And I'm pretty sure they know that you have been alive all this time." Her eyes widened at his words, but she didn't have any of her own. At her shell-shocked expression, Donnell continued.

"I've looked into their past, they used to work at the same hospital together, attending several medical conferences together, even before they were both married, and both of them are connected to someone else I'm not too happy about.

"Who?" Dustin asked before she could.

"Donna Fallon." Donnell said curtly. Nadia sat in complete shock. Donna Fallon was the wife of her former CFO, Brian Fallon, who'd been shot and killed by his wife. It had been Donna that helped her get the position she held now at Gateway. To learn that they all knew each other was a lot to process.

"That has to be more than a coincidence." Dustin stated more than questioned.

"It is, and that's what's worrying me. I also received some other rather interesting information."

"What is that?" Dustin asked.

"Camille Kerchel recently quit."

"Really?" Nadia asked, confused.

"Why is that information interesting?" Dustin also asked.

"She didn't give a notice or even a reason for quitting."

"And you find that interesting?" Dustin asked again, not seeing the connection.

"After the situation with Gateway last year, I'm pretty skeptical about everything that happens and everyone." Dustin nodded his head at Donnell's response. Nadia shifted, uncomfortable in her seat. Dustin must have picked up on it because he asked her what was wrong.

"Lyanne asked me to hire her." Nadia admitted.

"She did?" Dustin questioned.

"When was she hired?" Donnell asked, simultaneously as Dustin.

"Less than a year ago. Shortly after Ashiree's kidnapping." Nadia answered, and Donnell began to type on his keyboard.

"Did Lyanne tell you why?" Dustin asked Nadia while Donnell was reading something on his monitor.

"Just that she needed a job because her last employer laid her off."

"She couldn't hire her to work for Kyle's campaign?" At Dustin's question, Nadia rested back in her chair and thought. That actually made sense. Why not hire Camille to work for Kyle? She felt slightly naïve that she had never considered it before.

"Don't worry. I'll have all the information on Camille in a few hours." Donnell said, capturing both Nadia's and Dustin's attention.

"Can I do anything?" Nadia asked, feeling helpless. She wanted answers.

"Try to relax. We'll get to the bottom of this." Both Nadia and Dustin nodded and left shortly after. The ride back to her apartment was quiet. Nadia laid on Dustin's shoulder and breathed steadily. Dustin rubbed the spot on the back of her hand gently as their fingers were intertwined. It was so soothing, and she wondered for a second how such a simple gesture could be just what she needed.

Lyanne Franklin did her best not to slam her phone on the desk at her last attempt to reach Camille. What had that girl been thinking by quitting? She needed her.

"Rough night?" Leonard asked, coming into her office and closing the door.

"Camille Kerchel resigned her position at Gateway." She grudgingly stated.

"Do we absolutely need her there?" Leonard asked.

"Yes. Without her there, I have no one inside Gateway to watch Nadia."

"It's been twelve years, Lyanne. I don't think you should worry about it."

"I felt that way too until her long-lost husband showed up." Lyanne spurted. Leonard walked over and sat on the edge of the massive desk.

"What do you need me to do?" he asked, his eyes intent on conveying to her, he'd do whatever she wanted him to.

"I need to speak with Nadia."

"Calling her won't work?" He questioned.

"She's not even talking to Kyle." She said, standing and attempting to move away from the desk. Leonard reached out for her arm and brought her close to him.

"I can arrange for you to meet her?" Leonard said, slowly removing her suit jacket from her shoulders.

"You'd do that for me?" she asked, staring into his eyes as he began to unbutton her blouse.

"I'd do anything for you."

"I just need to give her a message." She whispered breathlessly as his lips began to caress her collar bone.

"What kind of message?"

"The kind that helps her to keep her mouth shut, should she ever get her memory back." Leonard looked back into her eyes as a slow sadistic smile appeared.

"Consider it done."

Chapter Sixteen

Dustin watched Nadia pace back and forth in her small living area. After returning from Donnell's place, Nadia immediately went to find her sketchpad and asked Dustin to look at her other sketches. She'd gotten the idea on the way back to her apartment that she might have sketched another image that could help piece together some of her past. He had nothing. Only several sketches of the storage area were clear.

"Are you sure you don't recognize any of the others?" She asked him for the umpteenth time in the last hour.

"I'm sure. The rest of the sketches are a blur." He said, watching as she stopped pacing and shuffled her heal back in forth.

"I hate this." She exclaimed, plopping down on her sofa next to him and slumping her shoulders.

"You're putting too much pressure on yourself."

"I just wished I remembered." She confessed.

"Why don't we order something to eat? Food always helps." He suggested. She looked over at him and slowly nodded. He tried to lighten the mood by suggesting Chinese and making sure she had ranch with her eggrolls. It brought a slight smirk from her but not the full smile he wanted. They ate in silence when the food arrived and watched the television absentmindedly. A news crew was covering an Event Gala in Downtown Houston. Dustin wasn't surprised to see both Dexter and Damien arriving with their dates.

"Aren't those your friends?" Nadia asked.

"Yes."

"They have really pretty girlfriends." Nadia commented. Dustin slightly chuckled. He was pretty sure the women on Damien and Dexter's arms were far from being their girlfriends. He reached over to her side table to grab a drink when he heard a slight gasp. Dustin's eyes immediately looked to Nadia, who was staring intently at the television in shock. He turned his head to focus on what caught her attention. Taking a moment to speak with the news crew was her fiancé Kyle with another woman on his arm. Dustin tried not the let the instant jealousy arise in him. He and Nadia hadn't discussed her relationship with Kyle. Naturally, he assumed there was no relationship. She must have felt him shift on the sofa because she turned to look at him.

"I'm sorry. I'm just shocked."

"I guessed that's understandable. He is your fiancé."

"I think him showing up to an event with another woman on his arm proves otherwise." Her voice was light in response.

"So, you're not upset?" He asked, knowing he bore a little resentment to her relationship with Kyle.

"About Kyle being with another woman? No. I guess I half expected it. Honestly, I haven't really thought about it. We haven't spoken since I left to go to the ranch." Nadia said, dipping the last bit of her eggroll in ranch and placing it in her mouth.

"Do you know the woman he's with?" Dustin asked, taking a swig of his drink. Her carefree attitude caused him to calm his momentary jealousy.

"Yes, her name is Margery."

"Were the two of you friends?" Nadia shook her head.

"More like acquaintances, at the request of Lyanne." Nadia said, standing to put away the last of her uneaten food. Dustin also stood and followed her into the kitchen. After throwing the items away, Nadia put the leftovers in the fridge, and Dustin tugged at her waist and brought her into his arms.

"I'm sorry."

"For what?"

"I get a little jealous thinking about you with Kyle." Dustin admitted. She leaned up to kiss him on the lips."

"You have nothing to worry about, but come to think of it, I should probably give him his ring back." Dustin smiled and kissed her neck.

"Yes, I think you should."

Leonard Franklin forwarded the calls from Kyle's phone after he responded to a text from Nadia. She wanted to give Kyle his ring back. No doubt she knew he was seeing Margery, as Kyle did not hide his new relationship from the public. Leonard smiled as she agreed to meet at a local restaurant. He placed the phone back on the coffee table as Kyle returned to the living room with two bottles of coke in his hands.

"I'm serious, Uncle Leonard. Mom's up to something. I know she is. I still do not know why she was so hell-bent on making things work with Nadia." Kyle said, handing a bottle to his uncle. "Nadia chose her husband, and things must be working out, considering I haven't even heard from her." He continued while taking a drink.

"Your mother just wants what's best for you." Leonard responded, Kyle scuffed.

"She just wants to control my life."

"I'm sure she sees it as guiding you on the right path." Leonard watched Kyle plop down on his sofa and practically roll his eyes.

"Well, you seem to reason with her when no one else can." Kyle complained. This time Leonard scuffed. No one reasoned with Lyanne when she'd set her mind on something. He hadn't known anything about the true nature of Lyanne wanting Kyle to marry Nadia until recently. Now that Kyle was determined not to oblige to that wish and somehow figured out Nadia Bolton was Tricia Hanson, Leonard was trying his best to deter his nephew from bringing unwanted attention to the situation.

"Hey Unc, do you mind if I borrow the limo tonight? My car is getting detailed and won't be ready until later. Plus, I kind of like the idea of not having my hands occupied while I take Margery out." Leonard smiled at Kyle's enthusiasm. He could admit Kyle seemed more relaxed in his pursuit of Margery than with Nadia. In all honesty, Kyle's request made his plan work out a little easier.

"Sure, Kyle. You can take the limo and enjoy your evening with your lady. I'll be happy to get your car."

"Thank you, Uncle Leonard." Kyle said, finishing the last of his coke.

Nadia checked her watch again as she waited for Kyle to arrive at the restaurant. He wasn't the type to be late, and she was certain he would call her if he couldn't make it. Texting him for the second time, she continued to wait. The waiter brought her another water with lemon, and she smiled, knowing he felt sorry that her date was standing her up. She was beginning to worry. After another ten minutes of waiting and texting Kyle again with no response, she thanked the waiter, apologized, and walked toward the front of the restaurant. The warm night air simmered as the moon now hung high in the sky as she stepped outside. Making her way to her car, she turned when she thought she'd heard something. A couple was walking toward the restaurant holding hands. The woman was leaning on the man's shoulder, and Nadia smiled at the pure love showing in the woman's eyes. She knew that feeling. Dustin. Lost in thought, she didn't see the black all-tinted Mercedes sedan pull up beside her. She breathed a sigh of relief seeing Kyle's car. At least she no longer needed to worry. She walked over to the driver-side window and frowned when the window rolled down and showed Kyle's uncle.

"Uncle Leonard?" she said, surprised. A man exited from the passenger side along with a man from the back seat. She took two steps back.

"Get in the car Nadia, I'll explain later." She looked at the man standing by the rear-driver side door, holding it open for her. The other man was slowly making his way in front of the vehicle from the front passenger side. Both men were tall, bald, and all black with shades on.

"What's going on? Where's Kyle?" She asked, not taking her eyes off the man in front of the car.

"Please, Nadia, get into the vehicle. I'll take you to Kyle." She took another step back. There was no way she was getting into that car willingly. She watched Leonard nod his head to the man in front of the car, he took a couple of steps toward her, and Nadia could see the weapon in his hand. Her eyes widened, and she turned instantly, attempting to run. She only made it a half step before she hit something hard. Something really hard. Lifting her head, she looked into the darkest eyes she'd ever seen. The man in front of her, also dressed in black, took her by surprise with a smile on his face.

"You seem to need some help." He said in a deep-timbered voice. Help? What kind of help? She didn't even understand what was going on. Was he trying to help her get away from Leonard and his men? Or was he helping Leonard and his men get her into the car?

"I don't think the lady wants to go with you." She heard him say to Leonard, stepping in front of her and blocking her from Leonard and his men.

"And just who exactly are you?" she heard Leonard ask. She couldn't see him, but she could see the man standing by the front of the car with the gun resting in front of him.

"I could ask you the same thing." The man helping her countered.

"Not that it's any of your business, but that young lady is my nephew's fiancé."

"Again, I don't think she wants to go with you." Nadia still couldn't see Leonard's face, but the man with the gun cocked it, ready to use it.

"That's cute. You're going to shoot me in the parking lot? You're not even smart enough to bring a silencer. That thing is going to echo for blocks. Not to mention the cameras in the parking lot." Nadia continued to listen as the man in front of her folded his arms with clear annoyance in his voice.

"What are you, some good Samaritan?" Nadia could only assume that came from the man standing by the rear-driver side door. The gunman had not spoken, and she knew Leonard's voice.

"I've been known to save a few damsels in distress in my day."

"We don't have time for this. Take care of him." Before Leonard's command could register in Nadia's mind, the man in front of her swiftly moved toward the gunman, catching him off guard, quickly disarming him and sending the gun skirting across the parking lot. The two of them tussled, distracting Nadia from the man by the rear driver's side door of the vehicle, who launched himself toward her. She turned to run away from him only to be caught by her arm. Attempting to twist away from him, she tripped, fell into a car, and hit her head on the pavement. She reached to touch the part of her head she'd hit. Squinting her eyes, she tried to stop the ringing in her ears. Her vision blurred as her protector landed two punches into her assailant's face. She wanted to cry out, to speak, to yell or anything. Tiny specks occupied her blurry vision as her protector kneeled beside her, as everything went black.

Dustin tried to tone down the rapid beating of his heart. Arriving on Nadia's floor, his nostrils filled with an antiseptic smell that always made his skin crawl. Ever since his father died, he tried to avoid hospitals altogether. The only exception was the birth of Dominic's son, Arion, and now. Rounding a corner, he spotted Donnell and a gentleman he didn't recognize standing at the end of the corridor.

"How is she?" Dustin asked, approaching them.

"Still unconscious."

"What in the world happened?" Dustin demanded. Donnell did a quick overview of the night's events, then looked over to the man standing next to him.

"Dustin, this is Malcolm Flynn." Dustin shook Malcolm's extended hand and eyed him skeptically.

"Nice to meet you, Mr. Shaw." Dustin nodded but turned his attention back to Donnell.

"What's going on, Donnie?"

"Flynn is a tail." Donnell replied.

"You had him tailing Nadia?" Dustin's throat almost croaked as he asked the question.

"No. Leonard Franklin, actually." Malcolm answered before Donnell could.

"You had a tail on Kyle's uncle?" Dustin asked.

"Yes." Donnell responded. Dustin quirked a brow at him, but before he could ask why, a nurse approached them with a clipboard in her hand.

"Are you Dustin Shaw?" she asked.

"Yes." Dustin confirmed.

"Your wife is waking up." Dustin's eyebrows shot up at her words. Nadia never referred to herself as his wife, and he never wanted to pressure her into that role.

"Thank you. What room is she in?"

"She's in room eleven, just here to your right." The nurse pointed to Nadia's room. "Would you like me to escort you in?"

"No, ma'am, I'll be fine, thank you." Dustin replied.

"The doctor will be back shortly to speak with you both." Dustin nodded, and the nurse walked into another patient's room.

"My wife?" He asked, questioning Donnell.

"I needed to keep this under the radar, so she's checked in as Tricia Shaw." Donnell answered. Dustin rubbed his hand down his face.

"You have some explaining to do." He stated to Donnell.

"I know, and I'll tell you later. Go check on her." Dustin walked over to enter Nadia's room. She laid in a slightly upright position with her eyes open.

"Dusty?" She called, catching him off balance. Nadia never called him that.

"How are you feeling?" he asked as he approached the bed. She instantly shot up in a panic.

"Whoa, whoa, take it easy, you hit your head." He reached out to her, but she flinched away from him.

"Who are you? You aren't Dustin." He winced at her words.

"Nadia, it's me."

"Nadia? Who in the world is Nadia?" Realization hit him like a ton of bricks. The fierceness in her tone, the brazenness in her voice, the skepticism in her face.

"Tricia?" He asked, almost scared to even accept what was happening before his very eyes.

"Of course, I'm Tricia, but who are you? Wait, are you Matthew or Jacob? Has something happened to Dustin in Mexico?" Dustin blinked, unable to believe what he was hearing.

"Trixie, it's me, I promise." He tried to reach for her hand again, but she quickly moved it from his reach.

"Don't call me that. Nobody calls me that but Dusty." She proclaimed in a louder voice than before. He saw her eyes squinch, and her hand attempted to cradle the side of her head.

"Hey, maybe you should lie back." He suggested. She did so reluctantly and eyed him suspiciously. He held back his smile. She was his Trixie, alright.

"I need Dusty." she said softly, closing her eyes.

"I'm here, I promise." She slowly shook her head back and forth, wincing with each turn.

"No, I need Dusty. He has to help her."

"Help who?" She slowly looked back over at him, straining to open her eyes. The big brown eyes that he'd loved since the first moment he saw them.

"Tara." She said above a whisper before passing out again.

"**How in** the world did you manage to screw this up, Leonard?" Lyanne scolded, sitting at her desk.

"None of us expected some military vigilante to interrupt us." Leonard answered.

"This isn't good." Lyanne stated.

"Can we find another way of ensuring her memory doesn't come back?"

"Short of causing an accident, no." Leonard rested back in his chair after Lyanne responded.

"We could lie low for a while." He suggested.

"You mean run and hide." She scuffed while shooting daggers at him with her eyes.

"I mean, take a step back and look at this from every angle." He countered.

"I've been looking at this from every angle for the last twelve years."

"What about Aileen?" He watched her roll her eyes.

"Aileen is about as useful as a box of rocks. It's been hard enough, these last few years, to keep her away from Nadia as it is. Plus, if anything goes down, she's going to sing like a canary."

"What do you want me to do?"

"Nothing. I'll handle it." She said, standing from her desk and walking over to her office window. Leonard knew he was being dismissed. He didn't like when she'd shut him out. But he would not badger her. If she said she'd handle it, he trusted she would.

Chapter Seventeen

"**Are you** sure she said the name, Tara?" Donnell asked, typing away on his laptop.

"Pretty sure." Dustin replied. His head still processing that Nadia woke up as Tricia.

"A last name might have helped." Donnell said casually, still looking down at his laptop.

"Sorry, I was kind of in shock that my wife woke up with her memory from twelve years ago." Dustin rubbed his hand down his face and leaned back in the chair outside Nadia's...well, Tricia's door.

"What did the doctor say?"

"That it's not uncommon after hitting her head that her memory could return."

"But she didn't remember being Nadia." Dustin shook his head. The entire situation was surreal. Spending two weeks with Nadia allowed him to see the woman he loved in a different light. Where Tricia had been bold and forthcoming, Nadia was reserved and uncertain. The contrast in their personalities was so clear, but his heart had taken to both. He could admit to himself, and he honestly hoped she'd get her memory back, or at least remember a glimpse of the love they once shared. The more time he spent with her, it seemed inevitable. Whether she was Nadia or Tricia, he would love her. Subtle similarities, other than looks, were evident as well. The doodling, the love for eggrolls, and preferring to dip them in ranch instead of duck sauce, but the biggest thing he noticed was her shuffling the heels of her foot when making a decision. For Tricia, it was a clear indication that she was ready for a confrontation at any moment. For Nadia, it was more of when she seemed to be unsure of a situation.

The question for him was how to find the balance. He wasn't the young boy he'd been when he'd met and fallen in love with Tricia. Yes, he'd spent the last few years of his life bringing the dreams of the life they wanted together to reality, but he wanted Nadia too. Remembering her eyes, as he mounted her on his horse. He'd been lucky enough to share that experience with her twice. With Tricia, she hid her uncertainty, faced whatever fear she had, and bravely stepped up to any task. With Nadia, she wore her vulnerability on her face, undeniably showing him she trusted him. Both occurrences filled his chest with pride. He loved Tricia's bravery and fearlessness, but he also loved Nadia's shyness and apprehension.

The clicking of heels brought him out of his thoughts as he saw Dominic, Ashiree and Shannon approaching them.

"Oh, my goodness, Dustin, how is she?" Dustin stood to greet them before answering Ashiree's question.

"She's stable, but she passed out again." They greeted Donnell as Shannon took a seat next to Donnell and pulled her tablet out of her purse.

"She woke up?" Dominic asked.

"Yes." Dustin answered.

"And as Tricia." Donnell added.

"What?" Ashiree, Dominic and Shannon said collectively.

"Yeah." Dustin said, rubbing the back of his neck and sitting back down again. Ashiree took the seat next to him. And Dominic took the seat next to her.

"Did she remember you?" Ashiree asked gently.

"Yes and no." As Ashiree's eyebrow lifted, he explained further.

"Oh Dustin, I'm so sorry. That must have been hard." Ashiree stated.

"I can't imagine. How are you handling that?" Dominic asked.

"Shocked and confused. She doesn't know me now." Dustin admitted.

"Whose idea was it to admit her in the hospital under Tricia Shaw?" Shannon interrupted, looking up from her tablet. It was hard to tell how Shannon's brain worked. Dustin pondered for a second on why she was there.

"That would be me." Donnell answered.

"Well, that makes my job a little easier." Shannon said while putting her tablet back in her purse.

"How so?" Dustin asked.

"The last thing the media needs is to find out that another Gateway employee was admitted to the hospital." She answered. Dustin nodded in understanding. He'd completely discarded all the drama that had taken place at Gateway Pharmaceuticals last year when Dominic took over. If his calculations were right, it was only ten months ago that they'd all been in this same hospital when Ashiree was found after being kidnapped.

"So, is there anything we can do?" Shannon asked.

"All we can do now is wait." Dustin answered.

"Would you like some coffee or something to eat?" Ashiree offered. Before he could answer, all of them turned and looked up, hearing two sets of distinctively rhythmic footsteps approach.

"What did you do, Sean? Go and find a twin." Shannon said. Dustin might have laughed if the situation had not been so taxing. That Sean and Malcolm walked in perfect rhythm made it clear they knew each other.

"Actually, I called for him." Donnell stated. He stood as did the others.

"Dominic, Ashiree, Shannon, this is Malcolm Flynn. He and Sean were in the same marine unit together. "

"It's a pleasure to meet you, Mr. and Mrs. Blake." He said, extending his hand to shake theirs.

"Nice to meet you, Malcolm." Dominic greeted.

"Call me Flynn, please."

"Well, Flynn, you can call me Ashiree." He finished shaking their hands and turned to Shannon.

"Ms. Walden, it's a pleasure."

"You also, Flynn." Shannon said, shaking his hand.

"I guess it's a good time for you to tell them why you hired Flynn to tail Kyle's uncle, Donnie." Dustin stated, shocking the others around them.

Nadia awoke to the beating sound of the monitor in her room. She had a pounding headache, and the beeping wasn't helping. Squinting her eyes, she reached up to soothe the ache of the bump on her head.

"Hey. How are you feeling?" She opened her eyes to see Dustin standing up from the chair in the room by the window. She instantly smiled seeing him.

"Hey. My head hurts a little." She admitted. She could feel a knot in the back of her head. Wincing again, she tried to sit up.

"Whoa, be careful, Trixie. You'll get dizzy if you move too fast."

"Trixie?" She said to him curiously. Was that a new nickname for her? And how did he come up with it? She watched his brows deepen at her confusion. Then, as if a light went off in his head, he closed his eyes and took a deep breath.

"I'm sorry...Nadia." He sounded disappointed when he opened his eyes to look back at her. She wanted to question him, but the doctor entered the room.

"Alright, Mrs. Shaw, It's good to see you awake again. How are you feeling?" she flinched at the doctor calling her Mrs. Shaw. She knew that she and Dustin were legally still married, but why would the doctor call her Shaw, not Bolton. She glanced over at Dustin, who seemed uncomfortable.

"My head still hurts." She admitted wincing.

"That's understandable. You took a nasty fall from what I understand."

"Yes, I hit my head falling in a parking lot." The doctor paused from looking at her chart and eyed her questioningly.

"You were in a parking lot?" The doctor asked.

"Yes, and a man was trying to attack me." Images flashed slowly in her mind of the incident. The men were trying to get her into the car with Kyle's uncle, another man coming to her rescue or at least she thought that's what he was doing. So lost in trying to remember what happened, she missed the doctor looking over at Dustin with a very questioning stare.

"That's interesting?" the doctor said, writing notes down in her chart.

"What is?"

"My nurse says you were in a car accident, and that's how you hit your head." She looked at Dustin, who still hadn't said anything. A car accident? She hadn't made it to her car. She also had not talked to any nurse.

"I haven't spoken to a nurse." At least, she didn't think she did.

"It's alright, you've been in and out of consciousness for the last couple of days, and with your head injury, a few things might be confusing at this moment. We'll run some more tests. In the meantime, I want you to continue resting." After the doctor left, Nadia leaned back in the bed and looked over at Dustin.

"He said I've been here a couple of days?" She questioned.

"Yes."

"How long exactly?

"Three days." She closed her eyes and took a deep breath. She didn't understand what was going on.

"Why am I checked in as Mrs. Shaw?" She asked, afraid to look at him.

"That was Donnie's idea. He thought it best. "

"Why?" It hurt to think, so she kept her eyes closed. It was easier to ask questions when she didn't have to focus on watching his reaction when he answered. She could hear the uncertainty in Dustin's voice, and it unnerved her. Why was he nervous? What was going on?

"We'll go over it later. Get some rest." She felt herself falling asleep, but she didn't want to. She needed answers. One answer in particular. She slowly opened her eyes to look over at Dustin. He'd retaken the chair and moved it closer to the bed.

"Who is Trixie, Dustin?" She noticed him shift uncomfortably in the chair.

"It was my nickname for Tricia." He answered. She wanted to nod her head in response but knew any sudden movement caused the pounding in her head to increase. Her heart almost ached at the knowledge of him calling her Tricia's nickname, but the doctor had called her Mrs. Shaw and said she'd talked to a nurse. She didn't remember any of that. An unthinkable thought entered her mind. Dustin said she'd been in the hospital for three days. The doctor said she mentioned being in an accident. Was it possible?

"Dustin." She softly called to him.

"Yes." He answered. She was almost scared to ask. Even more afraid of the answer.

"Did I wake up as Tricia before?" She watched him rub the back of his neck before answering her.

"Yes."

Donnell walked into the simple office building again, entered the elevators and waited to reach his designated floor. Once there, he again swiped his badge and was escorted to see the man behind the desk.

"I'm assuming you have something, with the urgency of this meeting."

"Yes, and you're not going to believe it." Donnell said, handing the man behind the desk a folder and taking a seat in the one windowed office.

"You're right, I don't." the man said, reading the report.

"Are you absolutely sure about this?"

"Yes." Donnell said with confidence.

"You're putting the rookies and the old heads to shame, Mason. It's a shame I can't get you to work full time." He said, putting the folder down on the tin desk.

"I like being able to pick my cases." Donnell countered.

"You got lucky cracking a case like this, that, I can't argue with." Donnell smirked at his response. He did get pretty lucky.

"What's the turnaround time on this?" Donnell asked.

"A couple of days tops."

"Perfect." Donnell said and then stood.

"Not so fast, Mason. I have a case I would really like you to take on." The man behind the desk stated. His tone showed that he wasn't suggesting much as he was assigning. Donnell groaned but took the bait.

"What kind of case?" Donnell asked.

"Money Laundering. Something right up your alley."

"Send me the info, and I'll see what I can do."

"You'll have it before you reach your car." Donnell nodded and left the office.

Dustin held Nadia's hand as authorities arrested John and Aileen Hanson. John came out of the house willingly handcuffed and barely looked over at Nadia standing next to Dustin. Aileen, on the other hand, was not so willing. The minute she saw Nadia, she wrestled against the men escorting her out of the house.

"Don't believe the lies they are telling you. They are not true. They are not true. You are my baby, my precious baby girl." she started to yell. "I saved you. I saved you... You have to believe me." Nadia snuggled under Dustin's arm listening to the rants of the only woman she'd known as her mother. Aileen's eyes flared as she watched Nadia ignore her cries.

"You were always so selfish. Always wanted your way. I saved you and gave you a better life than that a drug-addicted mother of yours would have. She didn't deserve to have two living babies when I lost mine. I saved you, you ungrateful little brat. I saved you." She continued to scream as she was practically carried into the back of the police cruiser. Dustin held Nadia tighter as the police cruiser pulled away with an angry Aileen still yelling from the back seat as they drove away.

"Well, that was eventful." Donnell said, walking over to Dustin and Nadia. "You two alright?" Dustin looked down at Nadia, who looked up at him simultaneously and nodded.

"Yeah, we'll be good. I'm just glad that's over." Dustin stated.

"Nadia, if you'd like, you can retrieve anything from the house that you'd want."

"Really? They're going to let me go in?" Nadia questioned.

"I pulled a few strings. I know there is still a room with some of your old things in there. I don't know if you'd want anything, but just in case you did."

"Yes. I would. Thank you." Dustin heard the true sincerity in Nadia's voice. They walked together, following Donnie into her childhood home. The two-story-style home felt bland as they entered the front door. An officer led Nadia to what he assumed was her old bedroom while Dustin looked around. This was where she grew up. The walls were painted an eggshell white, and plants stood tall in the corners of each room. Dustin noted the elegant rugs throughout the home. Donnell stood in the high vaulted ceiling kitchen, speaking to another officer. The coffee pot was still on, and the smell of coffee still lingered in the air. Dustin headed toward the hall. When he heard a slight rustling, he followed the sound to a bedroom he was sure had been Tricia's. The officer that escorted her to the room nodded and headed back down the hallway. A few boxes and a dresser remained in the room. A few bleached spots on the wall, where Dustin was sure Tricia had posters hung up at one point.

"Nadia?" He called out, not seeing her as he entered the room.

"I'm here." He heard her say from the closet. As he walked closer to the open closet door, she met him at the entrance.

"Are you okay?" He asked. She nodded.

"Did you find anything?" Dustin inquired.

"No, I thought, maybe if I looked around, something might stand out."

"You're putting too much pressure on yourself." He said, reaching for her waist and slowly pulling her closer to him.

"I know. Thank you for being here with me."

"Where else would I be?" He answered, smiling and leaning down to kiss her forehead.

"I hate to interrupt, but did you find what you might want to take? These guys are getting a little restless." Donnell urged.

"Yes, I didn't find anything." Nadia said. The three of them headed out of the house together. Donnell told them he would catch up with them later, and they walked over to a car, where a driver held the door open. Once settled inside, Dustin gave the driver directions to their destination and then looked over at Nadia.

"Are you sure you're alright?" Dustin asked.

"Yes, Dustin." She said, leaning over to kiss him and resting her head on his shoulder. They rode in silence as the sound of the car moving along the road echoed around them.

Chapter Eighteen

Nadia placed the last of her items from her office in a box. Opening the drawers on her desk, she double-checked to ensure she'd cleaned everything out of it. A knock on her door caught her attention.

"Kyle! What are you doing here?" She smiled coyly at him.

"I wanted to catch you before you left."

"Come on in."

"So, you're really leaving, huh?" She nodded. This chapter of her life was over.

"Yes. I'm ready to start a new chapter in my life." She stated proudly.

"I think that's wonderful." He said earnestly.

"Thank you, Kyle. Oh! I have something for you." She quickly remembered and reached over to grab her purse. She turned to hand him the ring. He smiled as he accepted the ring from her, putting it in the inside pocket of his jacket.

"So, what are you gonna do?" Kyle asked.

"I don't know, but I'm curious to find out." She said confidently.

"Well, I wish you the best, and I'm truly sorry about all of this." Kyle stepped forward to embrace her in a hug.

"It's not your fault. Life is full of surprises." She said, hunching her shoulders as he pulled away.

"Some better than others." He stated.

"What about you? Are you still going to run for the Senate?"

"I think I'm going to bow out gracefully. To be honest, this was the life my brother wanted, and after losing him, I thought I could honor him by making his dream come true." Hearing Kyle's words, her thoughts instantly went to Dustin. That is exactly what he'd done, honored the dreams, wishes, and promises to the woman he loved and lost.

"Well, I wish you... and Margery the best." She told him. He stepped back and nodded.

"Thank you, and I'm sorry about that." Kyle said genuinely.

"Don't be. I think I've always known she's had a thing for you." He smiled, slightly uncomfortable at her words.

"What about you and the cowboy?" He said teasingly.

"His name is Dustin. And we're working things out." She answered.

"I think that would be good for you."

"You do?" She asked, surprised by his encouragement.

"Yes. I hear the happiness in your voice. Three years of us being together, and I've never heard you like this. Plus, I've seen your face when you think about him." She looked up at him, trying to hide the slight smile forming on her face.

"There it is." He said, looking at her knowingly. She tried not to smile, but in trying not to, she smiled harder.

"See, I've never made you smile like that. I'm almost jealous."

"I'm sorry."

"It's fine. Mostly, I'm teasing, but it's true. There's something there, whether you understand it or not."

"It's just a few things I get nervous about." She admitted awkwardly. It felt weird discussing her feelings about Dustin with Kyle.

"What? Like a lifetime of memories that you don't remember." He teased.

"Yeah, like that." She said with a laugh. "And It seems weird getting relationship advice from my ex-fiancé."

"Maybe, but it's no different from me giving advice to my ex-fiancé." she chuckled at his words. "The thing is..." he continued. "...I've spent the last eight years trying to live someone else's life, and the last three, trying to ignore my feelings for someone else.

Knowing that everything was orchestrated and manipulated by my mother completely frustrates me. But I can either dwell on it or live better because of it. I choose to live better." He retraced the steps between them and kissed her on the forehead. "I hope you live better because of it too."

"I plan to." She said honestly, accepting his embrace.

"I hope I'm not interrupting." They both took a step back and turned to see Crystal Sands standing in the doorway. "I've been instructed to come and gather Ms. Bolton for her going away celebration." Crystal said cheerfully.

"I was just leaving. Take care of yourself, Nadia." Kyle said as he left her office.

"Goodbye, Kyle." She watched him as he left and noticed Crystal turning her head to the side, watching Kyle head toward the elevators. Nadia cleared her throat, getting Crystal's attention.

"Oh, I'm sorry, but that man was really good-looking. Was that the fiancé or the husband?" Nadia just shook her head and chuckled. That she'd even had both at the same time still astonished her.

"The ex-fiancé." Nadia answered.

"If the ex looks that good, I'm dying to know what the husband looks like." Nadia couldn't hold back her laughter at Crystal's playful attitude.

"As long as you see him with your eyes and not your hands." She countered, shocking the both of them. Where had that come from? She wasn't one to make bold statements like that.

"Well, excuse me." Crystal said, dramatically putting her hand to her chest. "It seems like you have grown a feisty side, Ms. Bolton." She laughed but didn't respond and followed Crystal to the conference room, where the rest of her peers gathered to say their farewells.

Dustin gently rubbed Nadia's back as she slept. The last few days were pretty hard on her. Realizing she'd awakened as Tricia sort of freaked her out. She didn't remember any of it, and she even told him she was scared that she might wake up as Tricia one day and completely forget who she was again. It was confusing listening to her ramble. She wasn't trying to make sense of it all. She just needed to share her thoughts.

The arresting of her parents hadn't set well with either of them. Finding out she wasn't even their child put an ugly stain on the entire situation. He'd held her all night as she cried, fallen asleep and then awakened in a fit of tears again. For two days, he'd taken care of her, making sure she'd eaten and stayed hydrated. It felt a little cramped in her apartment but there wasn't any other place he'd rather be than with her. After the stress seemed to wear off, she'd lain in his arms and shocked him by telling him she wanted to leave Gateway. She'd felt with everything that Lyanne Franklin and her mother tried to control regarding her life, she couldn't stay there any longer. Naturally, he invited her to the ranch, wanting nothing more than for her to be him. Nadia agreed after she'd thought about it for a while, understanding that if she found something else, she wanted to do or found somewhere else she wanted to be, he would support her.

Today had been her last day at Gateway, and most of the items in her apartment were packed. Dustin hired a moving company to bring her things to San Antonio. He suggested she'd fly back with him, but she told him she wanted to drive her car there. He didn't argue, although he wanted to. He understood the need for her to have some time to herself. He leaned down to kiss her cheek and slowly exited the bed. Grabbing his shirt, he left her room and closed the door quietly. Flynn was in her living room.

"Everything's all set for her to leave tomorrow." Flynn said quietly.

"Thanks, Flynn." Dustin shook his hand, finding some renewed faith in Flynn after what happened in the parking lot at the restaurant. He wasn't happy to know Nadia had been hurt, but once Nadia explained Flynn had taken down a man with a gun with very little effort, Dustin conceded to be thankful nothing worse had happened.

"Are you sure you can't wait another day?" Flynn asked.

"I'm pushing it close as it is. One of my mares is close to giving birth. I never miss when the foal or fillies are born. Plus, I know Nadia wants a little time to herself. The last two months have been crazy for the both of us." Dustin answered.

"Well, you have safe travels. I'll see that Nadia makes it to the ranch safely."

"Thank you again, Flynn."

"No problem." Dustin shook his hand again and left the apartment. Approaching the yellow Camaro, he opened the door and sat inside.

"Only you would need a ride before the crack of dawn."

"Good morning to you too, Dillon." Dustin said.

"Seriously, Dustin, what is going on at your ranch that you can't wait until a decent hour?" Dillon complained as he pulled out of the parking lot.

"I told you I could have called a car service."

"No, it works in my favor." Dillon said, changing lanes on the road.

"How so?" Dustin asked curiously.

"The last time Damien and I came by the Manor this early, Ashiree catered in every breakfast food known to man."

"Between you and Donnie, I don't even know how there is food left in this world." Dustin responded. The two of them had been the same way in college. He'd never seen two people eat so much.

"We Mason men eat a lot, but just thinking about how crisp that bacon was, I think I love that woman." Dillon sighed.

"Don't let Dom hear you say that."

"Please, he's too worried about Ashiree making Donnell brownies."

"I heard about that. What's going on with that?"

"Oh, you didn't hear." Dillon said. Dustin shook his head.

"Ashiree, Shannon and Kelsey had a girl's night, a little too much wine, and I'm guessing Kelsey asked Shannon which of us she'd date since she'd known us so long. I'm not sure who she picked, but I know, me stealing kisses from her when she would visit Dom on campus was mentioned." Dustin chuckled, remembering Dillon trying to get a rise out of Dominic by flirting with Shannon. Dominic was very protective of Shannon, but Dillon's shenanigans never bothered him.

"Then it came up that Kelsey had a pin-up of Damien inside her bedroom closet. You know Damien is not letting Darwin off the hook for that."

"I can imagine he's milking that for all it's worth." Dustin responded.

"Exactly, but anyway, Ashiree answered playfully, saying she'd pick Donnie, so Dominic banned her from making him brownies." Dillon said, laughing. Dustin just shook his head again. His friends were crazy, and he secretly loved it.

Nadia exited her car and looked around the property. She smiled as she saw Harper approaching to greet her.

"Ms. Nadia. It's good to have you back."

"It's good to be back." She said honestly. "Is Dustin here?"

"Yes, ma'am, he's working on some fences on the west end. We have a couple of new hires since you left. You can wait for him in the house if you want."

"Thank you, Harper." He said his goodbye, tipping his stetson. She watched him walk off and turned to walk into the house but then decided to head to the stables. She was never comfortable going into the stables with the horses when she was here before. She thought to herself that if she were going to embrace a life with Dustin fully, she would have to learn to love horses. Or at least learn not to be afraid of them. As she entered the stable, she saw six stalls. Three of them held horses with dark brown coats and one with a reddish-brown coat. The last stall on the right seemed bigger than the others. The barrier separating it into two was torn down, doubling that stall in size, with an opening in the back wall. She noticed there wasn't a horse in it. She frowned, wondering what this stall was used for.

She continued out of the other end of the stable and noticed a huge corral. She noticed the corral extended behind the stable, opening the double-sized stall as she walked further. Along the edge on the other side of the corral, she saw a horse grazing. The horse's head perked up, aware of her presence, and slowly began to trot toward her. The horse stopped inches away from the railing of the corral, and Nadia studied his bleak black eyes and dull charcoal coat. She walked up to the railing and extended her hand, palm held flat and waited without even thinking. Sure enough, the horse trotted the last few steps, placing his head on her palm, and she lightly scratched. Her breath caught in her throat as recognition flowed between her and the horse. She expelled a silent cry, unaware of the tears streaming down her face, as memory after memory flooded her mind.

"Hey, Puck." She said through teary eyes and shaken breath. The horse nudged her palm as she gently continued to scratch his head. "Look how big you've grown and so strong." The horse further nudged her hand and neighed as if understanding her words.

"I can't believe he found you. Dusty actually found you." She exclaimed, tears continuing to flow freely from her eyes.

"I promised you I would." Dustin's voice startled her as she slowly turned to see him behind her. Through teary eyes, she watched as he closed the distance between them. Looking up into those gray eyes, completely stunned. "Tricia?"

Dustin looked down at the woman in front of him in complete awe. When he'd run into Harper on his way back, Harper informed him Nadia returned. He'd first gone to the house, but Ms. Anita told him she saw Nadia walk toward the stables. Assuming she planned to walk to the Equestrian, he quickly paced around the stable, searching for her. He was rendered speechless when he saw a figure standing next to the railing of the corral. Puck was standing only a few inches away. Fear was the first thing to grip him. Puck wasn't friendly to anyone new on the ranch. It took months to get

Harper comfortable enough to feed him when Dustin wasn't on the property. He'd almost called out to warn her but didn't want to startle Puck. Deciding to approach the corral calmly, he nearly tripped over his feet in shock as Nadia extended her palm as if to call for Puck. A few seconds later, Puck placed his head against her palm. Moving closer, he noticed Nadia's posture. She wasn't nervous or skittish as she'd been before. And the moment he heard her call the horse's name, he knew it wasn't Nadia.

"I can't believe he found you. Dusty actually found you." Hearing her words confirmed the woman in front of him.

"I promised you I would." He said out loud before even thinking about it. He watched her slightly stiffen before turning around and locking eyes with him. A few tears were streaming down her cheeks as he closed the distance between them.

"Tricia?" He asked.

"Hey, Dusty Gray." She said, smiling up at him. His arms wrapped around her instantly, almost fearing that this was a dream. He felt her chuckle against him.

"I'm never letting you out of my sight again, woman."

"I might agree to that."

"You might, huh?" He said teasingly. She shifted in his arms, placing her arms around his neck.

"I missed you, Dusty."

"I missed you more, Trixie." He said, descending his head to kiss her. She moaned softly against his lips. Puck's neighing interrupted them, and they both looked over at the horse, who appeared to enjoy their subtle reunion. Tricia reached over to stroke the side of his head. Dustin allowed one of his arms to hold her while she rubbed the horse.

"How much do you remember?" He asked.

"All of it." She answered softly.

"When?"

"Just now, actually." She said, chuckling and wiping another tear from her face. "It's hard to explain. When I saw Puck, I don't know. It just all came back."

"Do you have Nadia's memories too?" He asked cautiously as not to upset her. When she'd woken up in the hospital, as Tricia, she hadn't remembered anything about Nadia. She nodded, rubbing her palm along Puck's neck.

"There's a lot going on in my head right now." He heard her say. That was an understatement, he thought.

"Why don't we go into the house so you can lie down." Dustin suggested.

"No." She responded while still stroking Puck. Dustin did his best not to chuckle. The one-word Nadia hadn't told him in the last month was no. Tricia used the word as part of her daily vocabulary. He stayed quiet, watching her continue to stroke Puck.

"I thought I'd never see you again." Dustin knew she was talking to the horse. She finally looked over and up at him. "It's like seeing this place in a whole new light." She continued.

"I'm glad you're able to see it." He said earnestly. It was his greatest wish, he thought would never come true, for her to see her dream become a reality.

"I still can't believe you found him. How did you do it?" She asked.

"Finding him was easier than I thought. The trouble was once he was here, he didn't interact with anyone. Even now, he still likes to give Harper a hard time. Don't you boy!" He said while scratching Puck's head.

"Thank you, Dusty." She said softly. He took the hand still holding her waist and gently stroked her cheek with his thumb. She leaned into his touch, slowly closed her eyes, completely enthralled in his embrace. He slowly descended his head and gently kissed her lips.

"You're welcome, Trixie."

Chapter Nineteen

"**Everything** is so beautiful here, Dustin." Ashiree exclaimed, taking a seat in the family room of Dustin's home.

"Thank you, Ashiree."

"He did pretty good, didn't he?" Tricia said, winking at him and taking a seat beside Ashiree.

"I tried Trixie." He said, winking back at her.

"I have to admit, it's pretty impressive." Dominic added, sitting in the love seat next to the couch Ashiree sat on with Tricia.

"So, how are you?" Ashiree asked Tricia, settling Arion on her lap with his pacifier.

"It's a lot to take in. Especially with getting my memory back." She took a breath, recalling everything that had happened over the last three months. She couldn't explain it. It seemed she was trying to deal with two different people. Her fierceness to speak up and be bold, countering with Nadia's reserve and calm approach. She was seeing a counselor to help her sort through it all.

"I'm sorry about your sister. Her name was Tara, right?" Ashiree asked.

"Yes, she was my twin sister."

"That's unbelievable. How did you find her?" Ashiree said.

"She actually found me." At Ashiree's quirked brow, Tricia continued. "It was my senior year, and we were given an extra credit assignment of doing a family tree. I honestly didn't need the credit, but I figured it would be pretty simple. I did DNA testing as a part of my research. My DNA somehow ended up as a match on a donors list. I guess I didn't read the fine print when I sent my DNA sample. Tara came to me, hoping to get me to agree to donate a kidney. She'd been on the donors' list for almost a year, with no luck."

"Did you know immediately that you were sisters?"

"I didn't, but Tara said her mother told her before she died that she never believed her twin sister died at birth. I honestly didn't believe her. I figured everyone has a twin, so to speak, but not literally. It's how we ended up on the freeway that day. We were coming back from a blood-testing center in Beaumont."

"How did this even happen? Did the Hansons adopt you?" Dominic asked.

"She was switched at birth." Donnell interrupted.

"People actually do that?" Ashiree asked, pulling Arion tighter into her embrace on her lap.

"In my case, yes, and it opened up a can of worms." Tricia stated.

"A big one." Donnell agreed. Tricia looked over at him and smiled.

"How much of this did you actually figure out on your own?" Ashiree asked Donnell.

"At the time, it seemed very suspicious that Aileen Hanson and Lyanne Franklin knew each other. The article I found was before Tricia was born. But what are the odds that your old colleague has a son engaged to your supposedly dead daughter? Researching John and Aileen Hanson, I found they lived a pretty simple life, but my curiosity peaked as I started to dig a little deeper into Lyanne Franklin. I still only had bits and pieces of information, and nothing was coming together. It wasn't until Tricia mentioned Tara's name that I could connect some pieces."

"Uncovering a child abduction scandal from thirty years ago?" Dominic asked.

"Yes. A closed case by the FBI." Donnell answered.

"Why did they close the case?" Dustin asked.

"I think they believed the person responsible was dead."

"Who?" Ashiree asked.

"A doctor named Ruby Kerchel. She worked in multiple women's prisons across the country, helping pregnant women that were incarcerated. A job most doctors didn't want and rarely paid much. She organized the adoption of the incarcerated women's babies to wealthy families without the consent of the birthing mothers.

"Did they find out how Ruby died?" Dominic asked.

"Yes. A brother of one of the women in prison killed her. He was looking for his nephew at the bequest of his sister, knowing she hadn't signed anything to have her child adopted. He found his nephew and discovered his adopted parents were sexually abusing him. He killed the adoptive parents, but not before finding out Ruby Kerchel set the entire thing up." Donnell answered.

"How did Tara fit into all of this?" Dominic asked.

"Well, once I had Tara's name, I found a missing person's report on a young woman, with that name, around the time of the accident. I noticed her birth date was the same day as Tricia's. It didn't send up any red flags at first. I figured I'd still look into it. First, I found an old yearbook album online with her high school picture, which put my curiosity into overdrive with their resemblance. I found it strange that Tara was a twin. The other twin, another girl, died shortly after being born. I then discovered that Ruby Kerchel signed Tara's birth certificate, and an old hospital report made by the mother claimed it was impossible. She never had any complications in her pregnancy, and both girls were perfectly healthy during her last checkup. She even tried to file a lawsuit, but no lawyer would take her case."

"Why not?" Ashiree asked.

"She was a junkie, and complications happen in pregnancy all the time."

"So, the hospital just ignored it?" Ashiree questioned.

"I don't think they intended to. It was a full moon that night, and over twelve different women gave birth within eight hours of Tara's mom."

"Including...my mother." Tricia interrupted, still in disbelief.

"If only the hospital had taken the claim more seriously." Ashiree sighed.

"It wasn't that simple, and the odds were against Tara's mother." Donnell responded.

"How so?" Ashiree questioned.

"The doctor, a nurse, a hospital administrator and a birth records supervisor were all involved." Donnell confirmed.

"So, Ruby Kerchel was the doctor, and I'm guessing Tricia's mom was the nurse." Ashiree stated.

"Yes, and Lyanne Franklin was the hospital administrator. But the kicker was the birth record supervisor." Donnell answered, and Dominic groaned, causing Ashiree to look over at him with a quirked brow.

"Who?" Ashiree asked.

"Donna Fallon." Dominic answered.

"Noooooo." She said eyes widened in disbelief.

"Donnie and Shannon worked a miracle to keep Gateway out of the media, again." Dominic said flatly.

"So, they all knew each other?" Donnell nodded at Ashiree's question.

"And Ruby Kerchel was Camille's mom, right?" Ashiree continued. Donnell nodded again. "It's sad Lyanne sent her to Gateway to spy on Nadia." Ashiree stated.

"Everyone has a price." Dustin added.

"What's the situation with Lyanne Franklin?" Dominic questioned.

"She lawyer'd up big time. Working on a defense to say she was unaware of Tricia being switched at birth." Donnell explained.

"Do you think it will work?" Dominic inquired.

"On that particular charge? Maybe." Donnell said, shrugging his shoulders and continued. "However, on the other charges, she doesn't stand a chance. Donna Fallon is writing a statement and willing to testify to the entire scandal to reduce her sentence."

"Well, our lives have just been full of adventure this last year, huh?" Ashiree joked and looked over at Dominic.

"I wouldn't want to share this adventure with anyone else, sweetheart." He responded, leaning over to kiss her as she happily met him halfway.

"Well, I don't share your enthusiasm, but I am happy it's all over." Dustin said, leaning down to kiss Tricia.

"I think I'll partake in some of the refreshments Ms. Anita has set out for us." Donnell excused himself as the couples embraced and made his way over to Anita as she slowly straightened the snacks on the table.

"Hello, Ms. Anita."

"Hello??..." She said, unsure of his name.

"Donnell."

"Ah yes, Donnell. Would you like a cookie?" She said as she placed it in his hand with a napkin before he could respond.

"Thank you, ma'am." He said as he devoured the entire cookie in one bite.

"Would you like another one?" She asked teasingly.

"I would, but I probably shouldn't." He said, slightly teasing her back.

"Can I get you anything else?" She offered.

"No. I'd actually like to talk to you about something."

"Oh? Alright, well, have a seat. You're quite tall and will give this old woman a crook in her neck."

"Sorry about that." Donnell said, taking a seat.

"Now that's better." She said. He nodded before proceeding.

"I am sure you are aware of the child abduction ring recently uncovered."

"I am. Dustin filled me in a little, but it was all over the news, so the story was hard to miss."

"Very true. But I discovered something else in my findings while doing my research."

"Oh?"

"Yes. One hospital had you listed as a patient there."

"Well, I'm not surprised. I spent a few years of my life in various hospitals around this country. Some, even out of the country, trying to find a cure for myself. I spent most, if not all, of my life savings, and low and behold, my saving grace came at a horse equestrian in San Antonio." She said with a chuckle. Donnell nodded.

"Dustin has told me your story, which I see as a miracle in itself. But my findings discovered something else."

"Really? What is that?" Ms. Anita questioned.

"Before your treatments and experimental testing, you were in the maternity ward of one of those hospitals." He saw her stiffen, then began to busy herself by straightening up perfectly placed items on the table beside them.

"You gave birth to a child Ms. Anita." He saw her hand still on the tablecloth as she closed her eyes and inhaled slowly.

"A daughter." He continued and watched her slowly look over at him.

"Did you find anything else?" She asked in a shaking voice.

"I did. I found her." He heard her exhale lightly as if she weren't aware she'd been holding her breath.

"You have?"

"Yes. And she's closer than you think." She hunched a brow and followed his eyes, and he turned his head slightly toward the others across the room. His eyes landed on Ashiree, handing baby Arion to Tricia. He was reaching for Tricia's nose as she tilted her head back, laughing, then placed him on her lap and gave him a pacifier.

"Are you sure?" She asked him quietly.

"I'm pretty sure. DNA doesn't lie." He said. Looking at her nod slowly, never taking her eyes off the two ladies and the baby interacting.

"Have you told her?"

"No. I thought I'd speak with you first. I wasn't sure when you saw her if some sort of maternal instinct would kick in." Ms. Anita finally looked over at him and shook her head.

"I never saw her." She admitted. Donnell nodded and stood. He gently placed his hand on her shoulder, and she lifted her head to look up at him.

"I'll leave the decision up to you."

"She has a pretty good life now. I'm sure my secret won't have the warming welcome I would have hoped for in the past had I found a cure sooner and been young and able enough to take care of her."

"Again, that decision is up to you." Squeezing her shoulder lightly, he grabbed another cookie and popped it in his mouth before rejoining the others.

Tricia leaned against Dustin and waved to Dominic and Ashiree as the black SUV pulled away. Their visit was cut short because Ashiree learned her best friend Chelsea had gone into labor. Donnell left yesterday after their talk. She felt Dustin shift behind her, and she turned her head to look up at him.

"Are you ready for this?" He asked. She nodded and watched as he picked up a brown bag that sat on a porch chair. She took his other hand as he led her to the stables. Puck bucked mildly in his stall but calmed the moment Tricia came into view. She saw Dustin shake his head. Puck had become putty in her hands. Together they walked to the lake that Dustin allowed her to name Gretel's Lake. Dustin held out the bag in his hand as they stopped at the edge of the lake. She reached inside, retrieved the plaque she'd made, and read the inscription.

"Tara Carver, may you always be remembered." She leaned down and placed the plaque against the bank. Digging a nice hole to secure it. She closed her eyes, remembering the woman who, had things worked out differently, would have been her sister. So much lost, so many lives affected, and so many lies told. She attempted to stop the flood of memories of first meeting Tara, the shock of discovering she'd had a sister, and that she had ultimately been stolen away as a baby. Kissing her two fingers, she placed them on the plaque.

"Goodbye, my sister." She said solemnly. Puck huffed next to her, and she stood, leaning into him.

"Don't worry. We didn't forget." She told him. Looking over at Dustin, who also smiled at Puck's impatience, and pulled a smaller bag from inside the brown one. She opened it to find white rose pedals. Reaching inside, she grabbed a handful and tossed a few in the lake. "To my beautiful Gretel. You are forever in our hearts. We miss you." She said. Dustin sighed next to her, slowly reached into the small bag, grabbed a handful of flowers, and tossed them in the lake.

"To you, mom, I love you, and I miss you." Tricia knew how hard that last summer at camp had been for them, first his mom, then Gretel, then Puck. But Dustin had kept his promise, he'd found Puck, and she was forever grateful for it. Together, they walked around the lake. Dustin stayed silent, except for a few chuckles, as Tricia talked with Puck about his mother, as she'd promised him, she would years ago. Later that evening, Tricia lay cuddled in Dustin's arms as his fingers lightly grazed up and down her arms. She almost laughed at the thought that entered her mind.

"Hey, Dusty."

"Yes, Trixie."

"You still have another promise to fulfill."

"Is that so?" Dustin said, smiling down at her.

"Yes, I seem to remember asking for a bunch of little crumb snatchers running around."

"Kids? You want us to work on having kids?"

"Don't you?"

"Of course. I just didn't think you'd want to start so soon."

"I lost twelve years with you, with us and our life together. I don't want to waste another second." A slow smile displayed on his face.

"Then let's not waste another second." He said, leaning down and capturing her lips. She accepted his kiss, expressing every ounce of her love for him. Basking in the knowledge that their love was timeless, it was priceless, and most importantly, it was endless.

Epilogue

Donnell Mason almost rolled his eyes, seeing Darwin calling him yet again.

"Yes, Darwin, I'm almost there." he answered. Trying to keep the aggravation in his voice to a minimum.

"I just want everything to be perfect." Darwin said nervously.

"It will be. Just relax. I'll be there in fifteen minutes." After Darwin calmed, they hung up, and Donnell attempted not to laugh. Donnell wouldn't have even agreed to pick up the treats for the birthday party Darwin was planning for his girlfriend Kelsey if Ashiree had been in town instead of visiting her best friend in Boston. He made a quick turn onto the service drive of I-45 and shortly arrived at the Grand Opening of the new bakery Branded Flavors. Parking his car a few spots down from the door, he watched patrons coming in and out, smiles and pure excitement on their faces. The bell on the door chimed as he walked in. The scent of freshly baked pastries, donuts and other delectable treats wafted in his nostrils. A low, appreciative moan expelled from his throat as he took his place in line. The baker was currently handing a little boy a cake pop with sprinkles on it. Donnell glanced around, noticing the décor in the bakery. Pictures of various food items were displayed on the semi-colored pink walls, and two-seater table settings were lined against the front window. There was even a small children's table set up in the corner.

"May I help you?" A voice called. Donnell's attention was drawn back to the line, realizing he was next. Approaching the display counter, his eyes connected with the bakers. Whoa. Her eyes were dark brown, almost as if made from chocolate. Donnell blinked at his odd thought. It wasn't a secret amongst his friends that he loved sweets or treats of any sort, but he'd never looked at a woman and thought of food. He took in her curvy frame covered by a red and white striped apron.

.   "Yes, sorry. I'm here to pick up an order for 'Knight'." He finally said.

"Sure, give me one second." He watched as she disappeared behind the double kitchen doors and took a moment to appreciate her backside. Voluptuous was all that came to mind. Glancing at the array of tarts in the display case, he noticed they were unlike any tarts he'd ever seen. Many were decorated in various themes like movies, sitcoms and cartoon characters. He was hunched down looking through the display case when the baker returned.

"Here you are! The payment has already been taken care of. Would you like a view?" He quickly stood to his full height as she placed the box on the counter and thought on her words. He would definitely like a view. A quick flicker in his brain reminded him she was talking about the box of treats. He felt his phone vibrate in his pocket and knew most likely it was Darwin calling again.

"No, I'm sure they're perfect. Thank you." He said, grabbing the box and turning to leave.

"I hope you enjoy them and come again." Her smile was warm and cheerful as he left and headed for his car. It wasn't until he placed the box on the passenger seat he smelled the scent of lemon. He smiled, knowing Kelsey loved lemon. Starting his car, he headed over to Darwin's condo, as the scent of lemon filtered its way through his car, and the Bakers' sexy chocolate eyes occupied his thoughts.

About the Author:

MzSassytheAuthor is a mother of three from Detroit, MI and currently living in Texas. Her love for reading started with book series like "The Babysitters' Club" in her childhood years. Most of her adolescent years were spent writing poetry, but it wasn't until her adult years that she discovered her love for writing, particularly connecting stories and reoccurring characters. She loves family and friend relationships and displays them in her writing. She enjoys traveling, attending sporting events, puzzles, and, of course, snuggling up to read a good book.

Thanks for reading! Please add a short review on Amazon or Goodreads and let us know what you thought!

Made in the USA
Columbia, SC
16 January 2024